STOLEN AIR

NIALL QUINN was born in Dublin. He has worked in the merchant navies of many nations: Britain, West Germany, Norway, Greece, Iran and others. He has lived and worked in South America, the United States, Bangladesh (where he spent a short while in prison) and in several European countries — a dishwasher at Scotland Yard; a factory worker in Hamburg; a barman in Salamanca; an air-conditioning installer in the U.S. His first published work *Voyovic, Brigitte and other stories* (Wolfhound Press) won him the Brendan Behan Memorial Fellowship Award.

By the same author
Voyovic, Brigitte and other Stories (Wolfhound Press, 1980, 1983; George Braziller Inc, New York, 1981)

STOLEN AIR

A NOVEL

Niall Quinn

WOLFHOUND PRESS

This book is published with the financial assistance of The Arts Council/ An Chomhairle Ealaíon, Ireland.

First published in 1988 by
WOLFHOUND PRESS
68 Mountjoy Square,
Dublin 1.

British Library Cataloguing in Publication Data

Quinn, Niall
    Stolen Air.
    I Title
    823'.974   [F]

ISBN 0 86327 157 X
ISBN 0 86327 158 8 Pbk

Cover design by Jan de Fouw
Typesetting by Wendy A. Commins.
Make-up by Paul Bray Studio.
Printed by Billings & Sons, Worcester.

"Whereas trees have roots, men have legs and are everywhere each others guests."

Portraits, Desmond McCarthy

THE HELMSMAN

AFTER A LONG and hopeless voyage the first sight of landfall is magical; it disturbs the mind. It promises release from the constraints and treacheries of the ship, and promises a new land of friendship and fulfilment. No matter how you know this, the first sight of landfall, after every long and hopeless voyage, disturbs the mind.

The pilot called, 'Starboard easy,' and a moment later shouted, 'Starboard!' The helmsman casually slipped the prongs of the wheel from hand to hand. The engines were running at dead-slow-ahead and a delusive silence filled the bridgehouse. For the first time in days it was possible to hear the sea lapping against the hull.

'Starboard!' Hard to starboard!' And the helmsman realised he'd been pushing the wheel the wrong way, towards the lights on the wharfs of Hueston and all their promise. He spun the wheel to starboard, tried to compose his mind against the coming rebuke, and waited.

'If you keep your eyes on the gyro,' the captain said, 'you can never make that mistake.'

The helmsman already knew this, staring at the gyro, knowing that a word of sorrow and a guffaw would dismiss the embarrassment. Or else the silence would alter its meaning, and turn itself into a challenge to the captain.

'It's the lights, Captain. The lights . . .' he whispered into the darkness, unable to continue, hearing each word strain against the silence, and so late in coming that they startled the captain. Without looking away from the gyro, the helmsman felt the pilot and captain exchange glances. From the back of the bridgehouse, from where the captain's wife and daughter stood, came the sound of carefully released, fat, female giggles.

The mistake had been commonplace, but not to a helmsman nearly seventeen years old and aboard his second ship, not to one who wished, above all, never to have to explain himself, or to apologise. Not, above all, to these people, to whom the sea was a profession, not an adventure. They brought their concerns for mortgages, wives, children, as pollutants to the freedom of the sea. They dressed themselves in uniforms and banished individuality. All the constraints and treacheries of land employment they brought with them. And to apologise to them, to explain himself to them, was a humiliating defeat for the last vestiges of his freedom. But these were his young years, the years of incessant defeat, and he carefully nursed himself from one defeat to the next, wondering how much more he could afford to lose.

A month before he'd been sailing on a tramp, a leaky and dangerous vessel dipping through the Caribbean and in and out of the hot and wild South American ports. But that boat lacked the hypocrisy of the regular, uniformed Merchant Navy, and had a steamy sense of fact and brutality. No one wore a uniform, everyone told lies, and no one asked questions. Where you came from was a place everyone had been, more or less; a condition and not a place, and what you did on the ship was what anyone on the ship would do if they couldn't get better. You were assessed and defined by much more subtle standards than your job, and the process took much, much longer than an interview or a voyage. Work was a curse, and with curses they laboured and wished it done. The whoring and drinking bouts were escapades to retrieve their individualities, and each fooled himself until each believed that the motive force of life was a dream, a dream shared with no one else, yet its substance forced the main part of each one's assessment of the other, and each recognised the untouchability of the other's dream.

All the bright lights on distant shores were merely so many street lamps on deserted, lonely streets, and cold enough to break any heart that believed in them. When the dreams faded with the passing years, or when cold, dreamless reality showed it too plainly to be unreachable, and alcohol, or something else, was needed to steady the hopeless hands and keep the eyes firm, as if one still lived for a life that had its passion, as if there was a purpose in enduring a life of no purpose, then no one held up the symptoms of life's disease as one's disgrace, or blamed one for being unable to live without a dream. If alcohol, or something else, gave one moments of respite from a hopeless reality, one found, then, that one also had the understanding of one's comrades, and belonged to their company.

On a drunken night, only weeks before, the helmsman had been musing on that into endless glasses of rum. When he awoke, dimly aware of the answers, they slipped away into nonsense and unconsciousness as he groped to fix their logic in his mind.

It was five o'clock in the morning and the barman, indifferent to the nightmares of sailors, was sleeping, in the gentle warmth of the tropical night, in a rocker on the veranda of the bar. A few tables further along the trampship's bosun was also asleep and a girl, with a superfluity of beauty and as young as the helmsman, rested against the bosun, patient and resigned even in her sleep.

Soon the bosun would stir, out of habit, and get back to the ship in time for work. He'd come ashore again in the evening, get drunk again, pay five dollars and take a girl upstairs, come down again, and drink and sleep the rest of the night while the girl patiently waited for another five dollars, or for drunken generosity.

.And so it happened. The bosun stirred and woke, put his huge arms around the girl, squeezed her, rubbed her breasts, gave her a loose dollar, and staggered towards the door. Then he pushed the rocker and woke the barman, laughed good-naturedly in the startled silence, and noticed the helmsman watching from the back of the bar.

'Work,' he called. 'Time for work.'

The helmsman had four months of work behind him, four months of working in the oppressive heat of the Caribbean each and every day; the common lot of trampship seamen.

Now he stared back at the bosun, wondering why the man was taking an inconsequential life so seriously. But the bosun was old, past thirty, an age when manual labourers ashore or afloat must find a niche where sweated labour is no longer required of them. And the need to do this, as the abandoning years leave them more and more vulnerable to the hurt and pain of inconsequential lives, leaves them impatient, irritable, even contemptuous and unfaithful, to those behind them who are placid and resigned to their fate.

The bosun stopped laughing, raised his clenched fist and shook it.

'Work,' he shouted. 'You come to work.'

The helmsman had two months' pay in his pocket, and already knew what he was going to do. He raised his open hand and made it quiver. The bosun sighed, and casually and powerfully tapped the watching barman on the shoulder.

'Get him a rum. Then send him back to the ship.' He turned and walked away.

It was normal. This was the honesty that pervaded the ship; not the ethic of work but its despair, the despair of work that was as satisfying as rock-breaking. Only the escape of drunkenness at work's end made it tolerable; the promise of the sweet fragments of thoughts and dreams before oblivion into the quiet escape of sleep.

'Please,' the barman said, 'you go to your ship now.'

So he too was frightened, more frightened than at thoughts of his own death. And these supernumerary fears were the greater part of him, and made and pointed his life. He smiled at the helmsman again, and again indicated the drink. Sometimes, on the ship, out of depression or bone-weary ennui, someone would lie-on of a morning and miss work without using the camouflage of illness. If he was tough and unafraid, and so untouchable, he was paid-off in the next port. Otherwise, in a fraction of time that scarred the voyage and became the essence of the voyage, hard, clenched fists, with a brutality that was slow-motional, punched into the man the despair of work. It was how the lesson was taught: that the man was there to serve the work. And by some similar dread the barman, without a memory of the lessons, remembered their ethics.

And, oh God, this wasn't the life the helmsman wanted.

Not at any age to find the world a place of despair and dread, and that despair and dread hidden and unspoken behind a list of duties that were collective acts of blind faith.

Back on the ship an act of submission would be demanded, an act or a gesture of suppliance to the secular ethics. Then the memory of the submission would sulk and disappear to the ordinary run of thoughts, for days or weeks or years, then re-emerge, like a childhood memory that re-appears for a second, and for a stunning second halts and paralyses with regret and guilt. Until memory is a quiver of such regrets and you walk carefully, throw no stones and avoid vibrations, for fear memory may hiss and its fangs strike and seize the present.

Already, from a too recent childhood, the helmsman had a stock of these fears, and nothing else, yet each fear capable of crossing his most intense moments, capable of separating them from experience, then pass away, leaving him dejected and curtailed of hope, aware of pleasant futures that his past denied him, aware that the mistakes of the past gave him little choice of futures. The future was defined and condemned by all the acts of shame and regret that sprung, as leering mockeries, into consciousness. The helmsman drank the rum and left the bar.

In the next street he found another bar. The females were the same mixture of stock as in the other bars, but here a placid Chinaman watched over them, forever ready to yawn at the most strange of requests, to consider, and to indicate the correct girl with the casualness of giving street directions. And then to yawn again, and go back to gazing beyond the world of human needs.

The putains sat, as decorative as potted houseplants, around the tables of the bar. Sometimes, out of boredom, they moved, to re-create their boredom in another place, and with their same indifferent awareness of it.

'You can have good time here,' the Chinaman said, after agreeing to the helmsman's request. 'Nice holiday.' And he smiled, his eyes holding the old adventurer's delight in watching the young scamper over his tracks. But these eyes took on a deeper examination when the helmsman bought a bottle of rum, ignored the putains, and went out back to climb alone the stairs to his newly rented room. He sat on the bed, lay back and touched one wall with his head, and tapped the opposite one with his foot. The room was windowless and dark, a section of corridor that had been partitioned into a run of putain-cubicles. On the floor, in a tray surrounded by pieces of coal, a small, red candle glimmered. Above it stood a plastic statue of a woman. After the second glass of rum he stretched himself along the bed and rested. This was peace. He slept.

Then he awoke, unstartled, in a pose he had never known before, his arms gently folded as he lay on his side, in the physical expression of his state of mind. And his nature had found, within the ramshackle bordello, a sense of security and peace, a sense of oneness with its world. So he lay and watched the cockroaches crawl around the dark walls. His eyes closed and for moments he remained smilingly aware of his comfort and ease. And in that condition he again passed into sleep.

The toilet was unlit at the bottom of a few steps at the end of the corridor. It was flushed with a bucket no one ever bothered to bring, and was choked with excrement. He felt the need to vomit when he entered. It was a deliberate, hard insult to his senses, and the thick, coiling smell followed him back along the corridor and into his room. He flushed his mouth with rum, spat it out onto the floor, then, recognising the armour he needed, he drank a glassful without desire or joy. He poured another and sipped it. From outside came the sounds of a putain coaxing a finished customer back along the corridor. When the rum raised enough courage in the helmsman, he opened the door and waited for a girl to pass. One did, bringing a Danish seaman to her cabin. She paused and looked in at the helmsman. '¿Bueno?' she asked.

He shook his head. 'Nada cigarette.' He held out a dollar. She smiled. '¿Americano?' He nodded his head. 'Momento,' she said to the Dane and went back down the corridor. The Dane staggered and entered the room. 'All the world,' he said, 'Norsk seamen, Spanish whores. And Swedish matches.' He laughed, pounded his chest, fell backwards onto the bed and groaned. 'I hate the sea,' he said.

The girl came back with four packets of local cigarettes. The helmsman noted the misunderstanding but let it pass as the girl spoke to him smilingly and softly in Spanish. Of all the words, as she repeated herself and simplified her language, a word sounding like timid came again and again. He nodded and said, 'Yes, timid,' and wondered if there was a difference between it and fear. The girl said, 'Nave no bueno,' then helped the Dane up with an easy professionalism and took him away. The helmsman waited, hearing the Dane and the girl groan and mumble and the wooden partitions along the corridor shake. Then they came out of the room, the girl in no way discomposed, and the Dane groggy with fatigue.

When they had passed by, after gently exchanging quiet salutations with him, the helmsman closed the door of his room and lay back on the bed. The noise of the bar below, with its many pleasures of the use and pursuit of money, sounded happy and uninhibited, freed from hypocrisy and its facade of convention.

Soon the bottle of rum was empty. The procession of feet back and forth along the corridor grew more and more frequent. The walls shook and groaned with the customers and putains in the sweat of the tropical night, the corridor a suburb of pleasures unmuted and unrestrained. In many languages curses, cries and despairing voices, and the sounds of smacks, rippled, unblushingly active, through the cubicles and the haze of alcohol, and hung, expressive of other things, in the hot, breathing air. And in that atmosphere of shaking, raw humanity the helmsman staggered to the door, asked a returning girl to bring a bottle of rum, swayed about the door until she returned, took the bottle, pushed the door closed with slow, studied, drunken motions.

Experienced seamen said it must be done this way, the only way to avoid the mandatory penalties every country imposes on seamen who desert their ships. But this way, drunk in a whorehouse, exempts you from the charge of deliberate desertion. And so, in the tranquility of a military peacetime, you hide your body in the slime and dirt of the city, and wait. Wait for the police to lose their immediate interest in you and pass on to other matters. And the alcohol helped, helped to kill time and to dull the fear of capture, the fear of being sent back aboard to work on a ship that must now hold the aspect of a prison.

He steadied the bottle on the floor, lay on his side half out of the bed, and snored into instant sleep.

Sometime later the door opened and a girl entered, the girl who had brought the cigarettes. She shook the helmsman, waited, shook him again, then rolled his unconscious body over to the wall. She sat beside him for a while, then lay down with him.

The helmsman turned over in his sleep, sensed the body beside him, and groped. The girl rubbed his face until his eyes opened and gazed, bewildered, at her. She too was afraid. Violence, even death, was a possibility from this unknown young male lying beside her. He smiled and released her, moved himself to the end of the bed, and sat there holding his head until the world refocused to its normal perspective. He reached for a cigarette, pushed off the bed, and knelt to light the cigarette from the burning candle in front of the plastic statue.

The girl screamed. She came from the bed and pushed him with all of her little might away from the candle, her face hysterical and beseeching as she moaned in despair, 'Mi amor mi amor, Madonna, Madonna.' She caressed the head of the statue and whispered to it. The helmsman watched, and understood, and closed his eyes. This was the girl's sleeping room, and in renting the room he had also rented her. She was obliged to tolerate his barbarian presence. He showed his open hands to her and shook his head slowly in a gesture explaining his regret to her. Her eyes closed and her head nodded in acceptance, and in weariness for the burdens of others that she had to share.

The helmsman moved the side of his hand in a cutting movement across his stomach, then he bunched his fingers and tapped them against his open, rounded mouth, enticing the girl as he would a child, while his eyes pleaded. She smiled a quick, abashed smile that left its warmth on her face, and nodded yes, she would like to eat.

Downstairs, next to the bar, they entered a large, facadeless restaurant, its front of doors now folded inside against the raised, sidewalk walls. Outside, in the soft, still air, the tropical insects buzzed in the night silence of the barrio. Odd seamen and putains sat and ate or slept around the wooden tables of the restaurant, bodies around a city campfire, and only steps away from the dirt road outside.

She touched the helmsman's hand. '¿Langosta?' she asked. '¿Langosta?' He nodded, wondering what it was. And the cook, seeing the exchange, poured a small amount of water into a large, oval pot on the floor, shook salt into it, then heaved it onto the range. The girl, chatting happily with friends, picked from the bowls of peppers along the counter, and occasionally turned to catch the helmsman's hand and smile and speak to him, delighted at his childish incomprehension. He smiled back, feeling relaxed and free in the soft, warm air, sensing the spaciousness of the great, wide South American continent, its vastness huge enough to swamp any past and to free the immediate future. And she, pleased now to be his, lightly radiant and happy, and pushing herself close to him with purposeful familiarity, her body tender and vulnerable and willing, an abundance of sweet, young legs, youth, and passion.

The cook pulled a heavy, canvas sack over to the range, shouted to an assistant, and together they raised the sack over the pot and pushed out two animals into the boiling water. The animals were large, as large as full-grown hands, with spiny, crusted, root-brown skin. The assistant clamped on the lid and held it with his weight as the animals bounced from side to side and the pot jumped in a frenzy on the stove. One tentacle slipped out under the lid. The cook wrenched it up and down and broke it off. Some drunks and others shouted '¡Olé!' and other cheers, until, after a few minutes, the pot ceased rocking on the stove. The cooks placed a small slab of rock on the lid and returned to their other chores. There was no awe. There was no sadness, not even an atoning respect to the animals for their gift of food.

The helmsman's breathing had become heavy and deep, and the girl, her personality raised in excitement, mistook the meaning of his heaving chest. She pressed one hand against it, and played with her fingers against the underside of his neck, her anxious mouth nibbling against the side of his throat. '¿Bueno, si?' she asked, and the putains and the customers nearby looked at him and her with some kind of admiration.

The sense of the world ceased. The cool night of the barrio, the warm skin of the girl, the sense of the bounty of the vast continent lost their continuation in him, and became trivial, external, the unsubstantial shadows of a fading dream.

'Rum,' he said without seeing the girl. 'Rum.' But she laughed and kissed him. She giggled and turned away in a step, her body swaying across her motion of travel as her feet gently and swiftly picked their places across the floor, every movement of her body and limbs an enticement of sweet legs and passion as she walked out onto the wooden sidewalk and into the bar next door. Her walk was graceful and free and young.

The ability to speak is learned by imitation. Thought, also, is learned by copying the reasoning steps and conclusions of others, and by juxtaposing them in a maze of cross references. Outside of this mirage is a beautiful desert of wordless incomprehension, and the juggling of others' thought into new constructs is no guide in its mystery. When a problem is not a clash of the cross references in the maze, but lies outside in the unknown desert, then it lies beyond the reach of juxtaposing thoughts, unless a violent clash of cross references produces an explosion, and a person gropes his way from the wreckage of the mirage and looks back, startled, at the behaviour of humankind. The helmsman was groggy, but transformed.

Teresa handed him a tall glass of Cuba-libre. He sipped on the rum and allowed his eyes to look once more at the weighed-down pot. And yet he must eat, must feed the body that gave him mobility and senses, the animal tract from mouth to stomach, the animal tract on the back of whose bosom interests he lived.

The cook used a meat cleaver to break open the shell-skin on the backs of the animals. Teresa carried the plates to the table, and fetched another glass of rum. The feast was good. She wrestled the white, steaming meat out of its jacket with her hands, licked her fingers and spoke copiously to the helmsman, took a sip of the helmsman's drink, and went back to eating. The helmsman watched her, hesitated for a moment, and then began to eat. The world was coming back. With each swallow of the food a new layer of relaxation and reassurance came over his body, and a renewed awareness of the lithe, brown body of the girl and its mating texture.

It was almost three a.m. The girls who hadn't been booked for the night wandered between the bar and the restaurant, nibbled at pieces of food, drank coffee, and eyed the flopped-out, weary drunks that sprawled about the bare tables. At worst these women were ungainly, but few were so. In all the South American ports the girls were recruited in the first flush of their mating bloom. They pressed forward, in ones or twos, to be recruited, and naturally took to their work with ease and facility, with alertness and animal freedom. By the age of thirty, or younger, they were gone. Some to broken wrecks loitering on corners, their passing bloom and charm gone without lasting reward. Many fled to death. Others found husbands and turned to house-tending and child-rearing, and disappeared into the normal run of housewives. And the interweaving cycles of nature, in blush and decay, pass onward without a pause.

The girl wiped her mouth with the back of her hand, smiled, and rubbed her small hands together. '¿Bueno?' she asked, and patted her stomach softly. The helmsman hesitated, and for a moment thought he saw a look of scorn or contempt for him hover about her eyes. It could be. He did not have a protecting and commanding presence. He lacked macho; that she had figured out with ease, so that look remained on her face. But it wasn't unkind. It had depth to it. She knew the American and European seamen often had a romantic attitude to sex, even when they were buying it, and often dallied shyly about the externals, made a dazzlingly suave ritual of them, and then copulated in a rough and rudimentary manner. Thereafter, the ritual was dropped, and they approached mating with quick and direct conjugal rights.

It was only of passing concern to Teresa, passing from the quirks of one customer to the quirks of another. She watched the helmsman, watched him visibly squirm from her probing eyes, and the judgements that flickered over her face. And while his eyes glanced away the helmsman sensed the intensity of the curious examination. Yet she was looking in the wrong direction, in the direction of masculinity and sex, and quite sure his deepest, twisting desires were hidden there.

The helmsman tried to smile at her, but failed. She seemed concerned and spoke and smiled at him, and her claustrophobic pressure on him increased. Alone, anywhere, the helmsman could have re-altered his feelings to a sense of peace. That was the supreme quest of his emotions. And Teresa, indifferent to such quests, and now in relaxed control of the situation, moved deftly to disarm the helmsman's retreating shyness, to bring him out of his unknowingness and mark him in the range of her experiences. When he began to speak in the demotic Spanish of the bordello her smile brightened and flowered with joy, for a moment. Then the hurt began to show. Her features gathered and tightened, and a loneliness grew in her eyes.

'¿No bueno?' she said, lost, and the question hung in her expression. The helmsman wiped his hands dismissingly back and forth, and the girl's anger flooded. Her voice and words rose into almost a scream and she gestured around the bar. But the cooks, the drunks, the putains themselves, were accustomed to face-saving displays from rejected clients and from rejected putains. They were part of the night's events that gave the barrio its atmosphere and character, and caused as much concern as the buzzing of the insects in the tropical night air.

The helmsman got up and walked to the side of the street. She followed, still shouting. He looked at her and she stopped, for a moment. He turned away, walked to the stairs at the back of the bar, and went to his room. There, in its emptiness and peace, he could feel remorse for the girl's hurt, and for the humiliation she must suffer to get another sleeping-place. He lay down and sighed, her concerns disappearing from his mind as his emotions re-ordered themselves into a sense of justification. He folded his arms and turned over onto his side. He closed his eyes, and at that moment the scene of the langostas fighting for their lives renewed itself with its original intensity. He sat up to shake the thought away.

It went, and left him contemplating the handful of flesh in his own head, the handful of flesh that was supposed to rationally govern him. It could not understand itself, nor explain its own workings to itself, and the helmsman laughed and shook himself, swore out loud, and lay back on the bed. He was almost one full day free of the ship, and already it was lost in an immensity of time, the faces and voices of comrades already disappeared. A soft, pleasant drowsiness came over him. He snuggled to himself and settled to sleep. This, as life, was sufficient, when the handful of flesh in his head did not fret and turn berserk, but went quietly and unpoetically into oblivion.

Outside in the night the abandoned girl sat on the sidewalk. The air was balmy and still, and the urchins in the doorways along the street slept contentedly. It was the only life they and Teresa knew, and in its context of birth and death they held no outside sorrow, nor observing joy, for it. They knew of no other context, not even the routines of day and night, only the periods between sorrow or happiness, before new demands of existence were made upon them and they turned, shy of the universe, and set to finding the bread or sleeping-place for the next day or night.

She rose, walked to the back, and climbed the stairs to her room. The helmsman was sleeping, and quietly she too lay down and slept. Bearing with such troubles as the helmsman defined life, gave it contours and flavours and made her feel both catalyst and mistress of the events from incident to incident. This time, when the helmsman turned and groped, she accepted him as naturally as a mother accepting her suckling child, and with the same poise of contented resignation.

She was gone when the helmsman awoke next morning. In the dirt and grime of the bed, in its soiled blanket, his happiness sparkled like a gem. He was free to lie on and not think, to laze and to enjoy that freedom more than the act, and to paternally reassure his nervousness and anxiety that there was no need to present himself for work. This was a habit that now fretted as an entity within him, an entity that forever threatened to take total control of his character. The helmsman moved and made himself enjoy again the feeling of the morning, the feeling of lithe, springing puppyness and play-fulness. Again he turned over in the bed and stretched. It was life in the grime of a barrio bordello, but it was free and fulfilling to his nature. And to reassure himself of that he had to reason to himself as if to a stranger.

The girl was sitting alone at the bottom of the wooden steps. The moment he saw her she rose and walked out of view as he descended the stairs. When he came into the yard she was standing in the brilliant sunshine holding a used cake of soap and a square of towel.

'Buenos dias.'

'Buenos dias.'

The taint of embarrassment over the uncertainties of the night disappeared in the gentle exchange of the morning pleasantries. Then Teresa gestured to the bucket of water and spoke to the helmsman in a manner of matured intimacy. The helmsman dipped his hands in the water and splashed some on his face. She laughed with delight and exasperation and spoke to the heavens in Spanish. From where he stood the helmsman could see the side-section of the bar and a section of the street beyond. He stepped back out of view and began to undress. She noticed the modesty and shook her young head in wonderment, and waited for the helmsman to soap himself. Then she raised the bucket and tried to swing it. A little water lapped out but fell far short of the helmsman. She spoke softly again, and again, then unexpectedly barked like a dog and the helmsman immediately squatted on all fours and the water sluiced out of the bucket, turned cold, and washed him down.

She went back to the steps and sat, unoccupied and uninterested, but proudly, while the helmsman dried and dressed himself. All other manners of life, even those that had been pleasing, seemed a childish waste of precious time. Life was exuberance and freedom, the grace of the sun on skin that was textured and vibrant with its youthfulness and pleasure.

The Chinaman, sitting small and demur behind the bar, smiled and nodded his head slowly, letting his eyes close and his face beam oriental benevolence and indifference. It was the face of the morning in the Caribbean sunshine as the putains and the urchins along the wooden sidewalk played sporadic games like boisterous young mammals learning their mock battles on the shore, then sat beside each other and rested, enjoying their unity and friendship. Housewives, and other representatives of a different order, moved with a mediaeval disdain through the streets of the barrio. Teresa never met their furtive, glancing eyes, nor looked at them. These people were sublime and aristocratic by assumption, and Teresa held the closed nervousness of those diffused and weakened by the class assumptions of others. Teresa held it close, as a personal disposition, without knowing it was the complementary emotion demanded by arrogance. And to

challenge authority that held such arrogance was beyond the
strain she could put on her nerves. Teresa acquiesced, as
sullen as a child in a lost street game.

The helmsman, undefined in the cloak of foreignness,
escaped judgement. And also in the bar and restaurant, and
from the other putains, the predatory deference shown to
passing trade disappeared from their attitude towards him.
And so the day passed in casual strolls around the barrio while
the girl spoke Spanish slowly to him as if he were a newborn
child, and added an answer to everything she said. They went
by the docks and he saw, with new-found nostalgia, the berth
where his ship had been, now rudely occupied by another
freighter.

Back in the barrio he bought spare clothing from the market-
stands. He gave the money to Teresa, indicated what he wanted,
and left her to bargain for each item. So they played as she
corrected his choice, as he objected, as they created a ruleless
game that their instincts knew long ago. Without the learned
illation of a common language, and through the barbed wire
of nationalities that separated their common origin, they
established a keenness of understanding that was unobstructed
and fluent as they harmonised their feelings for each other,
defined their context, and grew to communicating familiarity.
Even the European seamen wandering through the market-
place in the hard, flat sunshine of the afternoon seemed
removed from another experience, stood as aliens on a step
of evolution different to the helmsman's, and so alien that he
wondered how he had ever merged with them.

She, unconcerned with the trivialities of men, still led him
through the market in search of things to buy. He had all he
needed, yet she still dallied by the stalls. He gestured an
invitation towards the goods and smiled. But with the serious-
ness of buying a possession that must be lifelong, and must
dumbly serve purposes happy or sad, she checked the sturdi-
ness of a shiny, plastic suitcase, snapped its locks to and fro,
then quickly, and with the bland, bound face of duty, paid
for it and turned to walk back to the bar.

She was still serious and distant when they arrived. He passed
money into her hand and let her go upstairs to be alone.

The Chinaman served him a drink. 'Silly,' he said.

'Why silly?'

'You too,' said the Chinaman.

'Spending money you mean?'

'She wants to go to America, to the United States, California.'

The helmsman went upstairs, along the dark, narrow corridor, and knocked at the door of the room. When he entered into the solitude, the shining suitcase stood beside the plastic statue, and the girl sat on the side of the bed, mournfully staring at it.

'America?' he asked.

'Ah, si,' she answered, and moved herself on the bed to look expectantly at him.

'Mucho dollaria, Teresa, much dinero.' But he couldn't shake his head in warning.

'Ah, si, sir. America mucho dinero.' And she brightly smiled.

He thought of the bar downstairs, of the world of layabout days and nights, of the fellowship of the urchins and the putains, the buccaneer atmosphere of the barrio, and the fresh taste of a new and easy land.

Teresa watched him; he was pleasant and kind, yet one of the barbarians, and so much was within their power.

'¿Posible?' she asked.

'Si, posible.' And he turned and left the room, left the door hanging open, and found himself again at the counter of the bar.

'You told her you were American?' the Chinaman asked.

'No.'

'She says you did.'

'A mistake. I was talking about cigarettes.'

The Chinaman smiled. 'I'll tell her.'

'No, not yet. There may be a way.'

But it is never easy to get past the barbed wire, the concrete walls, the armed guards, and into the massive concentrations of money that bewitch the hungry and the ambitious the world over. And especially to those millions who live on the blunt edges of the wealthy, guarded citadels, who see the pomp and glory of the victorious television and the richness of the heraldic magazines. Close enough for that, but too far

away to see the sewers the castle is built upon, the never
ending rush to scale the slimy walls from the inside and to
find a niche of security away from other ambitious, climbing
hands. This was how those who came from such places of
wealth viewed them, yet only the deeply calm in the barrios
and coffee plantations shied away from such a vigorous, lusty
life. And Teresa was too young to be calm.

Sitting and drinking in the cool evening, separating himself
from the world, detaching himself from its concerns, the
helmsman could feel no more than the symmetry that the
procession of life presented. And it reduced him, as it reduced
everyone, to an insignificant spectator. He pressed back against
the wall and rested his feet on the table. The Chinaman
smiled. Everywhere life is cheap, cheaper than rice or grass,
and where it is most cheap it holds a feline awareness, and
grasp, of moments of happiness. And until she reached to
touch it, Teresa could enjoy the mirage of happiness. She
sat, preoccupied with herself, though idly relaxed and easy,
as if gathering and replenishing her emotions after an acute
crisis. Yet she cared in no way for this process, and let it
wash languidly over her. It was the way she survived all the
events of her life, from the moulding pressures of her recent
childhood to the abrupt dread and options of her adult life,
to the sadness at grief and the happiness at joy, without ever
knowing, as distinct, impersonal processes, the values she
responded to. As if knowing might disarrange the world beyond
her conception of sanity and leave her wandering in her mind,
alone, and forever rootless.

'¿Cine?' she asked indifferently, holding her head in her
cupped palms. She was beautiful and serene and the helmsman
pushed away the thoughts that verged on madness. Teresa
watched him for a moment, then comically distorted her face
and made him laugh.

They walked to the edge of the barrio where it met the area
of paved streets and domestic normality. The cinema was a
palace with wooden seats, narrow and short, and packed so
closely together that each body was squeezed between two
others. In the semi-darkness, pushing and easing through the
immense throng of people, they blended into the shouts and
noise and anonymity of the waiting crowd. There was a tense,

warm atmosphere of conspiracy before the movie started and drew them into its concerns. And the audience, sailors and their putains, and putains in groups, and other working girls and men from the shops, the guarded warehouses around the town, the guarded docks, and from the nearby coffee estates, all these people who had lost almost all of the bounty of joy of their birth, who were doomed by poverty to scavenge for livelihoods on the backs of industries that did not exist for their benefit, these people now subverted their concerns to those of the movie, became entwined and then transfixed by the characters. And for glorious moments of empathy they lived through the characters, and lived more fully than they lived their own lives. It was a movie theme as frequent and unchanging as church service. But the crowd rose out of itself in a heightened, collective emotion, shouted, cheered, murmured, worried, and gasped, as if breathing silently and deeply, and totally released and eased.

It was impossible to leave. The pack of the transfixed bodies was too great, and too enraptured in the movie, to be disturbed without danger. Moments before the end of the movie, without warning, the tension relaxed and a loosening developed in the crowd. Ones and twos at the back detached themselves and left, and before the movie finished erratic passageways through the crowd had developed. The helmsman moved to leave but Teresa caught at his hand, in the manner of a heroine, and demanded that they stay. It seemed intensely important to her, and her resolve was unalterable in the new set of her personality. So the helmsman, disappointed and confused by her profound strangeness, disengaged his hand and left.

The bustle of the barrio streets had moved indoors and very few poncho-clad figures moved about in the twilight. The occasional European-dressed men who wandered about nodded in greeting towards each other, exchanging 'good nights' and 'guten abends' that sounded odd against the solitary joy of the 'buenas noches' lingering in the air. And in the increasing intervals of silence a sense of loneliness grew, a feeling of having fallen from his imagined place in Teresa's world. Yet then it was Teresa who receded in the helmsman's conception of the world. The memory of her rejected antics in the restaurant, of the childishness of her suitcase dreams, of the proud-faced aspect of her stubbornness in the cinema, all these defined Teresa as an irritation that he would soon cease to notice.

In the restaurant he pointed to the pot of peppered beans, the diet of the locals, and to the grey, lifeless bread. The cook pointed to the sack waiting in the corner. Perhaps it was merely the extra price he wanted, and still holding the filled plate he pointed again towards the selections of meat prepared for the monied sailors, until the helmsman agreed to take a helping of short, fat sausages that had eruptions on their skins like raised, crusted sores. Then the cook smiled, called him 'comanchero', and wished him a good appetite. The helmsman's disappointment relaxed its hold and he smiled back. The world was not always a place of shadows that took their substance from vanity, then flickered away, leaving the innermost vanities exposed and betrayed. There was also the settled, predicable world of common friendship. The helmsman ate his food and returned to the bar.

'Or Europe,' the Chinaman said, 'Remedios would also like to go to Europe.'

'Remedios?'

'Yes. Remedios. Teresa is the name she uses for business. When she came here her name was Remedios, but the seamen didn't like it. I changed it to Teresa.'

'Practical.'

'Yes. Practical.'

A shudder of disgust passed over the helmsman. He turned his eyes from the Chinaman and looked out into the tropical night, its beauty dimmed and violently scarred by the barrio's poverty. Yet its atmosphere held a sense of security and confidence that was the source of Teresa's placid strength, and of her lithe willingness to go forward, bravely and undaunted, into any society. The helmsman had no such power. The barrio was a place of refuge, a place of nostalgia for a life that had dreams and passions. And in the barrio it could be faked. That was its glamour and attraction.

The helmsman drank moodily, never aware of what his eyes saw, until again his eyes caught the sad, pensive stare of the Chinaman. It seemed as if the Chinaman was waiting for him to reach a certain state of mind, a conclusion, but turned quickly away when he saw the helmsman's pondering look. And so the predicament that was forming in the helmsman's mind received an oblique confirmation for a moment. He took the glass and the bottle of rum and went upstairs to his room, aware that he was a slow, dim learner, and whatever his feelings absorbed had to struggle and fret before coming clear in his mind. He sat on the side of the bed and drank. Teresa and the Chinaman seemed to know of a set purpose to life, and they pursued it quickly and easily, without doubts and without reflection, straight to its conclusion. They could never understand a void of purpose in any life, nor understand the pull of its vortex into despair. Boredom was their milieu and soon became their essence. The helmsman slipped deeper into drunkenness, stretching in the increasing ease of the relaxed present and the unwatching solitude of the dark room.

She stamped her feet and yelled, her two hands coiled into small, trembling fists of rage. She waited till his eyes squeezed open and took in the scene before kicking the empty bottle across the tiny ruelle, away from the statue it had rolled against. It hit the steel leg of the bed and broke. He lay and watched her for a moment then turned towards the wall. She screamed again and to regain her silence he turned back to watch her. She stamped her foot and became silent, then mumbled something, sighed, and left the room.

He tried to sleep. She started talking to someone directly outside the door and he called to her to stop. She carried on, and he shouted her real name. She stopped, for a moment, then carried on. He banged with his fist on the wooden partition. She opened the door, spoke some odd words gently to him, smiled, then returned to talking to her friend. The door stayed open. The groans and rutting noises along the corridor were at the level of the crisis hours, and in the midst of it Remedios and her friend were discussing the private life of a movie's heroine.

He fixed his stare on the burning candle beneath the blue and white statue, and waited for her to enter the room and close the door. When she did so she stood and watched him for a moment, then softly touched his face. He continued to stare into the candle's flame. She sat beside him, became very small, and brought her face to the side of his neck. The tip of her tongue tingled in his ear.

'¿Que pasa, Marinero?' she whispered. '¿Que pasa?'

He moved his face away and gestured towards the statue. She smiled warmly, held herself forward and reached for it. She cuddled the statue to her, a reassuring palm across its back. 'Ah mi amora,' she beamed at the face, 'pobre Madonna,' and hugged it to her breast like a doll, without shame or self-consciousness, but with an abundance of love. She squeezed the statue to her and looked up. '¿Comprendo?' she asked. He shook his head. '¡Ah!', she said, and went back to caressing the statue and rocking herself back and forth on the side of the bed.

'Remedios?'

She paused and looked at him for an instant, then reached and put the statue back against the wall. 'Si,' she said, 'momento.' And a moment later she smilingly laid herself along the bed, supine, a gentle, young mammal fluent and relaxed in the play of nature, her ensemble of emotions as shadows in the overture. Yet vigour and force were indelicate to the helmsman's tenderness for her. She smiled at him and prepared herself for him, speaking softly and enticingly. He touched the brown, textured skin and the sweet, quickening passion of her legs, then lowered his mouth to her womb. This was the source and care of modesty, the holder of fidelity and the place of trust. Her hands caressed his head, and her legs moved in slow pressing movements as she silently eased out the crisis of emotion. This was the quest of courtship and the lovers' bond, and this the guage of immorality. He felt her emotions slacken and she lay quietly, still fondling his head. He laid his head on the warm, pure skin of her stomach, and slept.

Sometime later she tousled his hair and awakened him. 'Langosta,' she said, and smiled, before her smile began to break into laughter and she turned away, and silently smiled at the world. The helmsman lay naked in the heat of the bed, squinted past the light, and tried to re-match Remedios to his previous image of her. She had a haloed expression of contentment.

She seemed aware of this, and when they dressed she took his arm as they walked along the corridor, descended the wooden steps, crossed the yard and the bar, passed along the sidewalk, and entered the cafeteria.

The helmsman turned away while the animals were being placed into the pot. Remedios giggled and caught at his arm. She would not take this revulsion seriously. She put a finger on his lips, spoke gently to him, and happily answered herself, then freely swaggered away to fetch a bottle of consoling rum.

They drank from the same glass and waited for the food to arrive. Organic matter now inorganic, the carrion that sustained life, bred life anew, fed from it again, until the world was a molten mass that devoured itself, regurgitated itself, the devoured and the devouring merely changing places in the continuously chewing maw of nature. But there was no way to arrest the essential processes of life, nor to change them, and the helmsman and Remedios ate and drank in a keen and concentrated manner.

Towards the end of the meal the helmsman noticed that Remedios was watching him, watching him as if changing the visual background from one scene to another, and comparing how he fitted to each. It was a mature, serious examination of him, and when he shifted, uneasily, and inwardly growled at it, Remedios was also suddenly surprised at what she had been doing. An aura of confusion and embarrassment came over her. She anxiously gathered the plates and brought them back to the counter, then dallied there. The helmsman waited. The post-midnight busyness of the cafeteria had ceased, and only a few clients, returned from their visits to the suburban corridors above the bar, sat about drunkenly at the tables.

Remedios wandered over and sat beside him, and for a little while her presence created an oasis of calmness against the unsettled questions between them. She said, as a casual remark to ease the silence, that the night was always more beautiful than the day. The nights were the times she liked best, from the nights of her childhood in another town, and in those nights she escaped to the cocoon of her bed and the endless fantasies of makebelieve where she saw herself becoming, night after night and in all manner of ways, a Catholic nun who saved the world from many dangers, and brought many fallen men back to Jesus Christ.

Remedios smiled. And once, too, she had been a nurse

bringing succour to men dying on battlefields all over the
world. Only a handful of years ago she had dreamed these
things, and they still had a place of respect in her understanding of the world. Yet now a home and children would
be of more content to her nature, but she knew it was just
another dream and appropriate to her age.

She pretended, with her hands flatly together, under the
side of her face, to fall asleep on the helmsman's shoulder.
And immediately the import of her naivety became clear to
him. Remedios casually reached for the almost full bottle of
rum and refilled the glass. Now that the avowal was over it
was time for activity and girlishness to deflect the ready
embarrassment. She took a sip from the glass and then handed
it to him. The forced simplicity of the language, and the trite-
ness of the examples, were necessary gestures to his lack of
understanding, but also a demonstration of her commitment.

And to have the fate of a human being so nakedly in his
hands was unbearable. There were so many better men in the
world, men with money and power and a prosperous future.
The helmsman drank to that, and Remedios laughed a little
highly. The barrios of Europe were cold slums of material
poverty and spiritual degradation.

'Ah si si,' she said, she knew, but America had many beautiful places for new people. But he had no skill that would buy
him admission to that country, he could not go there, and
Remedios' face began to darken with betrayal and disappointment. And in Europe he was poorer than she was in the barrio.
'Ah si si,' she said and exhaled a sigh. She reached for the
glass but it was empty. She refilled it and gave it back to the
helmsman. She was beautiful and in many other ways also
much too good for a seaman who had only enough money to
live for a few weeks in the barrio.

Remedios pushed the back of her chair to the wall and
turned away from him. It caused the conversation to fall like
a broken limb between them. And the casual noises and talk
of the cafeteria flowed into the growing silence. He took the
bottle and wandered out onto the sidewalk, walked a little,
then squatted down derelict against the wall, in the total
peace and sense of the night, and drank.

It would have been easy to sleep then, to let his head

fall back against the wall and to slumber as deeply as a child, to blissfully forget the care and consideration Remedios demanded, to let it slip from his concern. To forget.

He tipped the bottle up to his mouth but no liquid came. He let the empty bottle roll away across the sidewalk, and watched it hesitate on the edge, then languid fall into the dirt road. It seemed part of the pleasure of the night and he chuckled to himself, pulled the small, flat moneybag from under his shirt, and peeled some dollar notes loose from the bundle. He was rich yet, and for perhaps a fortnight at this rate. And he was stupendously alive, drunk, and thirsty. He stumbled down the street to another bar, entered, paid for a glass of rum, and when the interest in his drunkenness seemed to have evaporated in the watching eyes, he bought a bottle and staggered back out onto the street, and almost as far as the safety of the cafeteria's light that beamed across the wooden sidewalk. Just before it he squatted and tipped the bottle to his mouth. His handling was faulty and some rum slopped onto the front of his shirt. He rubbed it dry against his skin and instantly forgot about it.

An Asian seaman walking past stopped to ask if he was alright, then walked on. It caused a sense of self-consciousness to stir in the helmsman, and he felt a need to demonstrate his rationality, his conviviality, his ability to dismiss the alcohol, and to behave with a great and reassuring reasonableness. The alcohol merely helped the pupa to blossom, and its brief, butterfly nature sparkled the amused eyes of the Chinaman who sat and endured the flood of reminiscences and confessions that flowed past the helmsman's unguarded mouth. And when the urge to explain cleared itself, the helmsman found his hands roughly massaging and twisting the empty bottle before him. The Chinaman's eyes closed for a moment in consideration, and he moved his head slightly as if an understanding had been reached. It was a benevolent gesture, and relieved the helmsman of his anxiety that some unbecoming guilt had been confessed.

The street and the night and the bar had passed into pre-dawn quietness. Around the bar the putains and the clients were isolated and asleep in the stillness. A groan, or a snore, or a blind pushing movement from a sleeping body, caused a ripple of broken sounds, then all was quiet again. Gently, with drunken concentration and meticulous, slow-motion gestures, the helmsman padded past the bodies, pulled himself up the stairs and along the corridor, quietly opened the door, and discovered that Remedios had left. The suitcase and the little statue were gone. For a moment it numbed him. Every corner of the room was visible, but in disbelief he called her name. It was the right room, and her absence from her place in it disordered the entire world. The great burden of his love for Remedios pressed on him once more, and for the first time he was conscious of what it was. Then it fell away, and he was aware of a feeling of release. He sat down on the bed and stared at the empty room, and at his re-ordered universe. He laid himself along the bed, wide awake, turned on his side and moaned in a luxury of tiredness, reached out and felt the empty space beside him, and went to sleep with his arm across it.

A girl was sitting outside the cubicle door next morning. Alert and smiling wide-eyed at him, she squatted in so agreeable a manner that he smiled back, and was bewildered that a feeling was missing in the exchange. When he said, 'Buenos dias,' his voice shook nervously. The helmsman was dishevelled and dirty, and scratched disinterestedly at himself and at no particular irritation as he walked down the stairs.

As he crossed the bar the agitation of his body became greater, and with difficult and deliberate pressure he forced himself into a posture of relaxed camaraderie with the Chinaman. The Chinaman gave him thin slices of lemon. And between sipping small amounts of straight rum he chewed on their bitterness. He watched the steady hands of the Chinaman pour another minute measure into a tall, long glass. It was tall and long so that the helmsman's shaking hand could grasp it in a fist, and manage it to his mouth. But his body tried to refuse at the mere taste of the alcohol, his head turned sharply and shook itself, and he had to massage the back of his neck to relieve the tension. Gradually the process induced a pattern of deep, languorous breathing, and a growing feeling of bodily calm. The rum regained its pleasantness, and relaxed the helmsman's rigid concerns. Without thought, he dried his juice-wet fingers in the cloth of his trousers. The Chinaman was refreshed and as brightly clean and new as the radiant tropical morning. The measure of control he held over his life was fully exercised, and he said the helmsman should do the same. Push away the tentacles of others when they started to bind him. Otherwise there would be nothing left of himself for himself. It was the female's function to bind a man, and to pull him down to nest. Many men liked this, and functioned with assurance and purpose because of it. Remedios wanted a home and children, and the rearing of children. The helmsman's place was obvious, if he wanted it. And he would merely have to chase around the town to find her.

The helmsman and the Chinaman laughed and smiled. At the same moment the helmsman was conscious of the Chinaman's glancing eyes and, immediately, the presence of nearby women. The helmsman froze, then huddled lower against the side of the bar. The women didn't speak English, but in their very alertness they seemed to have sensed the betrayal and subversion. The Chinaman chuckled and walked away. And it was the surprise of that, and after a startled effort of reflection, that made the helmsman aware of his own defensiveness, and of his instinctive assumption of it.

He hadn't slept long, and over the last few days he hadn't eaten properly. There were many reasons for the raw vulnerability he felt. There had been never-ending scenes of shock ever since he entered the barrio. The frenzy of the langostas going to their deaths still lived in him, as the least of many realisations, and of Remedios' gentle frenzy to awake him to her, and of his never-ending habit of being, forever, one step behind his own understanding. Always one step too late to alter his own life, and to fully exercise his measure of control over it.

He looked at the Chinaman sitting quietly at the end of the bar. Then he refilled his glass, chewed another slice of lemon, straightened his back and sipped from the glass, his steady hand now properly managed. The girl who had waited outside his room was sitting a few seats away, still waiting. An air of indifferent, languid patience covered the entire bar and made the helmsman feel distinct and out of place. The girl smiled at him and he looked away. There was a feeling of captivity and observation. And then the helmsman realised that he was talking out loud to himself. Every act and facet of his life gathered and trembled into that one moment, then disappeared into its void. Getting up to leave the bar and to walk into the street were acts of creation in a new world. Every emotion and movement rang as if new and untested.

The chasm around his thoughts lessened slightly in the street, but the fear continued to flow into his stomach and around his body like blood. It effortlessly pierced the shield of alcohol and held full prominence in his brain. He pushed on through the thick, watery air that slowly defined his movements in the street. And somewhere in it his former self, his former state of being, had disappeared. In it too was the raging fear that his body would dissolve in panic. He checked himself and stopped. Outwardly he looked profoundly struck by some unknown thought, and to himself he tried to reason that he was weathering the attack, that the worst that could happen was of no importance, that he could avoid its rigours by becoming an enthralled but detached spectator of himself. For a moment he almost resettled calmly into his former self, but the vitalities of his dreams rebelled against it and he thought he would faint. He turned back towards the bar, his eyes flickering open and closing the world in non-continuing, non-contiguous states of existence.

In the bar he saw the bottle on the counter, grabbed it, and violently shoved his way to the safety of his room. When he closed the door the strain in his mind eased. Whatever the price, even if insanity lay at the end of another drunken sleep, the unendurable wakefulness had to be ended. He tipped the bottle back to his gasping mouth, and immediately recoiled at the taste. Yet the delirium seemed to be ebbing. He sat on the bed and examined the bottle in his hands. It was a pretty bottle. And its silent confederacy with him was unquestionable. He rubbed his fingers across its neck and whispered to it.

The door opened, and again a surge of panic poured into his stomach. But the new girl, calm and placid as a nurse, ignored the position he was in and handed him a small open, brown bottle. It was from the Chinaman, and he cautiously raised it to his nose and sniffed it. The slight smell of cocoa stung his need for nourishment and food. He sipped the mixture, thinking it was cocoa, but it had a lighter consistency and flowed softly and evenly into his body. It was tasty and compelling. He sipped it again, and again its sweetness flowed into every fibre of his being. Then he was falling, as if from an unknowable height, wide-eyed but calm, and yet still falling, his eyes still open, into an abrupt and soft gathered fur of sleep.

He awoke from the calm, stilled sleep a day later, all his senses coming back into being smooth and unruffled. The contentment was deep and unshakable. In the backyard he shaved himself for the first time in days, washed, and hummed as he sluiced himself down with the cold, playing water. He walked straight-backed and relaxed into the bar, caught the Chinaman's questioning eyes, and laughed.

'Thanks for the cocoa.'

'Cocoa?' The Chinaman laughed and slapped the counter. 'Cocoa!'

'Wasn't it cocoa?'

'No. It wasn't cocoa.' His eyes swept casually over the helmsman, as if sensing a mood. 'It was a homemade medicine, nothing special.'

The helmsman walked on through the bar and around to the cafeteria. There were never very many customers in it during the daytime, and he slowly, with impeccable enjoyment and consideration, ate a fresh langosta for breakfast. Then he strolled along the streets to walk off the heaviness. The morning air was as cool and as tangibly refreshing as water. He walked down the sliproad to the docks, wondering if the unusual calmness of his nature would last.

A few sailors were lazing on the poop deck of the first ship. He cupped his hands around his mouth and shouted to them. But they didn't know if the ship was short of crew. They answered with heavily nasal, British accents. He walked on, a little embarrassed. As he passed by the gangway a short, fat man hailed him from the deck.

'Are you in trouble?' the fat man asked.

'Yes,' he shouted back.

'Come on up and I'll take you to the skipper. We're short here.'

He climbed the gangway. Walking along the main deck the man questioned him. He told the oldest story, of a drink too many and a girl too soft, and his ship long gone before he resurfaced.

'Always letting us down,' the fat man said. 'I'm Irish too, but I'm the bosun and the captain trusts me. Wait here.'

A few moments later the captain came out. 'So, Paddy,' he said, pleasantly, 'fall asleep on the nest, did you?'

The helmsman knew what was required, and smiled slightly.

'Yes, well, jolly good. Mr O'Flaherty here says you're alright, and you're quite young, aren't you, yes? Still it's highly unusual for us to sign on casual crew.' The captain stopped and waited.

'Yes, sir, I understand.' The helmsman spoke when he noticed the pause.

'Still, we've lost a lot of men in the whorehouses ourselves, and we're quite short, so I'll give you this chance.'

'Thank you, sir.'

'And for goodness sake use a sheath next time.'

'Sorry?'

'Fall asleep with that on and it curls back on the hairs. Skins you both alive down there.' It was said with such panache that the helmsman had no time to reply before the captain turned and walked back to his cabin.

The bosun and the helmsman turned to walk to the crew's quarters. 'Now you see what they think of us,' said the bosun, 'when we let ourselves down.' The idiom meant in that strange Irish sense startled the helmsman, but it was not the time to say anything.

'It's a respectable ship. The senior officers have their wives with them and we have poetry readings every Sunday afternoon.'

The helmsman thought of Remedios and the Chinaman, and of the resignation and calmness his nature had learnt. 'I have to go back ashore,' he said.

'Not at all,' said the bosun, 'not at all. Tell the captain the name of the bar and he'll have the agents fix the bill. We can dock it from your pay later.'

'Sheltered life here, isn't it.'

'Oh yes. Very comfortable. You'll like it here.'

Again the image of Remedios came to him, her longing, and her rolling white eyes, and the dream that flickered like sunlight across her anxious, waiting face, the dark hair that fell in wisps across the brown, textured skin of her shoulders. The sweet legs and passion of Remedios.

'It tasted I remember like lobster.'

'What's that?' The bosun stopped walking, bewildered.

'It's a line of poetry for Sunday afternoons when I'm old. How long to the next port?'

'Four days,' the bosun answered in an obedient manner. 'Hueston.'

Before lunch the helmsman signed ship's articles. The afternoon turned into a blind, dull struggle to return to the rigours of work. And before nightfall, with all the cargo loaded, they closed and battened down the hatches, and waited for the tide to flood. Then they let go the ropes and steamed out onto the Caribbean sea.

It was a pastel clear night with a distant ribbon of cloud in the untroubled sky. And the nymph-blue sea lay as calmly as fallen silk. The blinkered maze of lights ashore lessened to points, and one by one went out.

Going for'ard to the bridgehouse to take the wheel for the midnight watch, the helmsman stepped aside to let the captain's wife pass.

'Oh, I say,' she said, 'you must be the great romantic adventurer, aren't you? And her limp wrist and her limp head hung to one side as her concentrated eyes examined him. He smiled slightly, nodded, and rapidly passed on. The non-deliberate phoneyness of everyone was more and more apparent, as if they had been exquisitely mesmerised into stilled facets of themselves, dimensional, but as clearly cut for a limited purpose as a primitive tool. Whatever sense should have told them this was silenced, and left them hallowed and emptied of natural life.

The captain was on the bridge, checking the ship and the course before turning in for the night. He was relaxed, pleasant, and convivial, and bantered a little with the watch officer and the helmsman about the deceptive attractiveness of women. He had read somewhere, he said, that sex was nature's compulsory act of adoration, and all the denials and sublimations were wrought inlays on that act of adoration. The captain said it with an air of indifferent sadness, and looked out across the quiet, hushing sea. For a little while there was silence, as if each knew the adoration would never cease its demands, and never understand them as they understood it. It seemed an unfair and humiliating circumstance for reasonable men. The captain's wife entered, and at once the mannerisms of all altered in a rush of imperceptible degrees, and broke their silent bond. The captain was unaware of any change, and when he said goodnight to the watch officer and the helmsman, this loss of comradeship gave his manner an unconscious and straightened formality.

The watch slipped by in the routine of work, and the days fell in the same stoic pattern of thoughtless work, and the escapes into the unremembered dreams of sleep.

Sunday was the second last day of the voyage. In the afternoon the poetry reading was held, an affair of sturdy, dauntless women, and middle-class seamen. The portholes and doors were open against the heat of the day, and through the companionways came the voices of so many Sunday afternoons, the voices of school and the voices of church, without sadness or joy, mere voices that obscured the words they spoke and left a gaping, wounded sense of mysteries that were lost too long ago. A small patter of applause followed into the void. And still unaware of the already lost, another voice spoke into the tranquil, Sunday air, and urged itself to rage against the coming of the night.

Later, the sounds of biscuits and tea, and the smell of gin, came through the companionways.

That was yesterday afternoon. The pilot's instructions became more rapid as the ship neared the wharfs of Hueston. Again the helmsman heard the lure of the female giggles breaking from the darkness at the back of the bridge. A sensation of fear started in his stomach, then evaporated. Land and freedom were so near again. The pilot called for midships, stopped the engines, and had the aft guy-rope swung across to the dock. The for'ard ropes followed, and the vessel eased and nestled alongside the quaywall. It was the end of a voyage, and the voyage had no memory of sweetness or passion. It was a long and hopeless sleep between lands, it would vanish from memory, and leave memory to Remedios, to the Chinaman, to the magical experiences that disturb the mind.

'And sometimes we just gaze at you in joy for it delights us to see you here: a European among the whites'

Attila Josef on Thomas Mann's visit to Budapest

NA-V-'NAD

THE CAMPFIRE WAS burning by the side of the road. It was untended. I had no interest in its warmth, but huddled down to it for company. It had been a lonely day, and finding this fire brought an eeriness to my feelings. The countryside was shelterless and empty. A small bundle of twigs and branches lay near the fire, and I wondered what had frightened away the tramp.

I held my hands to the glow of the fire and waited to feel the nervousness of the eyes examining me from somewhere in the bush. The countryside was quiet. I closed my eyes and listened. Immediately all the sounds that my sight cut off became audible. The campfire roared. The light wind on the dirt road, and the invisible sway of the foliage, became sounds that were conclusive to the dying day, and included me, peacefully, in their end. In the feeling of that acceptance my sense of anxiety ebbed. I stretched myself alongside the fire, pushed my folded plastic bag under my head and settled, calmly, to sleep. Then I heard the tramp move. Perhaps it was the lull of my senses before sleep, or perhaps it was in the nature of the man as he moved through the bushes, but I felt I had nothing to fear. I turned on my side and watched him approach.

'Hija,' he said, as if he'd been expecting to find a stranger at his fire. He stood and looked at me on the ground. 'God-damn,' he said, and laughed, 'watch a man settle round a campfire and sure as hell he puts his back to the east.' Then he squatted beside me, and patted my leg, and I thought oh Christ. 'Relax,' he said, 'relax,' and went and squatted at the other side of the fire.

I had been alone for three days, and for three days I hadn't eaten. But the hunger had spurred me on, had made me walk in a determined, concentrated manner. My concern was not for food. I was consumed by a blankness of mind and by a certainty that my mind was working towards a conclusion and needed me to help it by walking rapidly and fixedly and by ignoring it. I could not recall a thought.

The man at the other side of the campfire was an intrusion into that obsession. My mind was calmly bewildered by the solidity of his existence and every normal reply that occurred to me seemed unreasonable and was dismissed before I could open my mouth.

'My name's Samuel,' he said, 'I own most of the land around here.' And instantly I synchronised back into normality. Every tramp invents a dream, and dreams it when he's asleep and awake until it totally blocks the reality of his doom. Not his doom as a man, but his doom as the character he is in his dream. But only in his dream. His dream dooms him, and what he is as a man can never accept that, and the man he is can never be helped, unless you appeal to the man he dreams he is.

'I'm sorry for trespassing, I said.

'Hell the damn state owns the road —' He stopped, and for a moment his gaze refocussed on my face. 'Let me tell you something about the law in this country, Mick.'

'Fuck off!' It was a nervous reaction. I was illegally in the United States, and I was stung to realise, again, that my accent so easily betrayed my origins.

Samuel looked away, towards the setting sun, and I saw a sadness and a disappointment on his face. He turned back, looked at me again, then looked into the fire.

'A woman called me Yankee once,' he said, 'like that. It stung like hell.' His hand went up and plucked at his eyebrows. 'That was in Europe just after the war.' Then he lowered his hand and smiled at me. 'You were still in diapers then, right?' I smiled and nodded. 'And now,' he said, 'you're a goddamn regular Na-v-'nad.'

I hadn't heard the word since I was a child in Ireland, and I smiled happily back, flattered, at his idea of me as an aimless wanderer. I was pleased that I even had some books in my plastic carrier bag. And while I was smiling at him I realised that he was appealing to my dream of myself.

A quick and total sombreness froze over me, but Samuel seemed unaware of it. The easy benevolence of his nature still passed across the fire. But there it fell, blocked out, by my sudden coldness. I was in the wrong place in a fixed distortion of reality. The past three days were being emptied of their value to me, and the night ahead, and my place in it, were passing into another man's control. And I was lying on the ground, propped on one elbow, and watching it all happen. I stood up and started to dust away with my hands at my already-over-soiled clothing. But the effort needed to set out walking again, after this respite, seemed mountainous, and I carried on dusting at my clothes. It didn't help. I stopped doing it and sat back down. It was a slump into self-pity, and I immediately consoled myself. I knew that acts of control over my life were expedient delusions, and belief in them was more suited to idiotic tramps like Samuel. The lack of food had given me a hypnotic confidence in my own judgements, and I lay back and stared at the darkening sky, and felt a very human well of sympathy for myself, and a pity for the lifelong stupidity of Samuel. I decided to tease the old, deluded fool. Perhaps it would perplex him into self-absorption, and the situation between us would be altered back into its proper perspective.

'Samuel,' I said, 'you come from the seed of your father.'

'Goddamn!' he said with concern in his voice. 'What's the hell's wrong with you boy?'

'But the seed of you was not in your father when he was born.'

'Jesus!' he said, and seemed bewildered.

'So where did he get your seed from, Samuel? Tell me that. Where did your father get your seed from, hmm? He must have ate, Samuel. Maybe he got your seed from a hamburger.'

Samuel was patting the top of his head with the open palm of his hand. Then he drew in a breath and exhaled a long, dispirited sigh. He laid himself out flat on the ground beside the fire and ignored me. And it was then I realised that he had no knapsack, no holdall, no bag of any kind, that he was clean-shaven and washed and that his clothes looked fresh. The twilight had settled, and re-examining him by the camp-fire light was unreliable. But memory brought back every detail. I had not consciously noticed them. My expectations of him had been fixed from the moment I saw him coming from the bushes and buttoning up his fly. Now I was equally sure that my memory was correct.

Samuel remained silent. I tended the fire with twigs and scrubs, left an airvent windward, and lay back down. At least I had perplexed the old fool into silence.

I almost fell asleep, but memory perplexed me.

'The Interstate Freeway's about six miles east of here,' Samuel said into the semi-darkness. I was indifferent and tried to be carried on towards sleep. I had stayed away from the freeways, deliberately. They made walking monotonous and tiring, and made me conspicuous to the patrol cars.

'When they're not busy at night, and most nights they're not, the patrol cars cruise around the back-roads.' I knew this too, and that was why I always tried to avoid walking at night. I wanted to be peacefully asleep under a hedge.

'You listening?' Samuel asked.

I pretended to snore, and he started to laugh.

'You better come home with me, Na-v-'nad, before they hear that strange, foreign voice tramping around without a permit.' There was nothing wrong with his accent, but something was out of place in the way he spoke. It wasn't the amusement in his voice. The amusement wasn't at my expense. It was comradely, affectionate, and full of the ease and peace that the man exuded. It came to me easily across the fire and it was all I needed.

The next thing I knew he was shaking me awake. The night had grown fully dark and the campfire had burned down to embers. My sleep couldn't have been very long, but I was restored and fresh.

'Come on,' Samuel said in a whisper, 'my place's just up the road.'

I looked into his face. I had a dim, unformed affection for the man, but I didn't want to fraternise, again, with any man, under the terms he was offering.

'Go get your boys where you like, Samuel. I'm staying here.'

The first look of anger came over his face, a concentrated, controlled violence that set his features and stilled the air between us.

'I am inviting you to my home,' he said, 'what the hell do you think.'

I was still curled in a sleeping posture on the ground, and he was stooping over me. Any movement meant an immediate, snarling fight. And his position was too good. Yet again it was the way he spoke, the way he used his words, that occupied my attention.

'OK Samuel. I'm sorry. I didn't understand. What would you have thought in my position? Christian charity?'

'Goddamn,' he said, 'I'm a married man with children.' Then he seemed to ponder what he had said and the anger passed from his face. 'I mean they're adults. My children. They're adults.' But he was still pondering as if the contradiction had just occurred to him.

'Sure,' I said, and laughed. 'You're used to taking fully grown strangers into your home.'

Samuel sighed and let the remark pass over him. I took the chance to uncurl myself and stretch. When he didn't react I stood up.

'You've got a dirty mind,' he said quietly. I wanted to laugh at his naivety. A man who could call adults children, and couldn't dismiss it as one more trick that language played on logic. I didn't know what language was native to Samuel, but I knew now it wasn't English. A tramp wouldn't analyse his sentences if he was speaking his native language. I was standing now and looking down on Samuel standing at his full height. I must have been gloating at the triumph of my petty reasoning. A look of disdain and disgust came across Samuel's face and he looked as dangerous as a snarling dog. But no more so than a dog. A few kicks and his courage would desert him. At worst I'd have to kick him to death, and it was only the tedium of doing that that dismayed me. It would be a boring, exasperating exercise. I had no feelings of dislike or frustration towards Samuel, and tried to alter the expression on my face.

'You're alright, Samuel. But you're old and your head is gone. How you keep yourself clean I don't know. But you're a road bum. Maybe you got lucky and got a shave and a wash and some fresh clothes somewhere today. But that's all. Then you wake me up in the middle of the fucking night and ask me to go home with you. You're not safe to be around. Can you understand that?'

'What age are you?' he asked in a quiet, sombre voice.

'I'm seventeen, Samuel. Does that excite you?'

He shook his head in disappointment and the anger left his face. He said I was two years younger than his youngest daughter, the only child still at home. I closed my eyes in despair at the strength of the man's delusions.

'The world is getting real dirty,' Samuel said.

'That's it. Now you've got it. Just hang on to that.'

'There used to be companionship on the road,' he said, 'decent men.' And the stupidity of this remark made me turn and walk away. The fellowship of the road is not bonded by the victory howl of a train passing in the night, nor the hooting of a steamer as she pushes out to sea. These sounds excite nostalgia when you're sheltered, warm and fed. They mean nothing to a tramp. The only fellowship on the road is bonded by alcohol, or other drugs, or sex, and they all end, when there isn't enough of any bond, with beaten, snivelling men curled up on the ground. There are the odd characters who are always aware of this, and they are the best companions. Samuel, the fool, was being romantic. And then I knew where Samuel's great air of peace, and also his exuberance of violence, came from. He was deranged, and wandering in and out of dreams, not as tramps and other people do, but as a simple lunatic. And sick as this world is, and despite my childish selfishness, I couldn't leave that senile old man to face the night alone in the open.

I turned and walked back. He was still standing by the remains of the fire, standing and watching me. The embers of the fire were lying in heavy ash, and when I crossed them with twigs they smoked briefly, then smothered the fire completely. It is these little things that destroy me, when the trivia of my judgement and of my ability is made most apparent by my inability to cope with the most simple things. I looked up at Samuel, expecting to see him smirking. He looked concerned for me, and disappointed, and again it was comradely.

He seemed to know the despair that a trivial failure could cause, seemed to sense it, and to know it made me re-examine the value and the worth of every judgement I had ever made. These simple things rob me, in an instant, of all my certainties. And Samuel was ready, without doubt, to share with me the despair that tightened every feeling in my mind and body. I knew it. And I also knew why a particular assumption governed all of my reactions to Samuel.

Weeks before, in New Orleans, I had been penniless and hungry. All day, and far into the night, I passed bar after bar, and by accident and in a daze I entered a particular bar. I noticed first the strangeness of the atmosphere, and then that there were no females in the bar. That helped, for women never look at a male without judging him. And I most desperately did not want to be judged in this position, and in the act of asking for the most miserable of charities. I went to the far end of the bar, into its most darkened spot, and sat alone at the curve of the bar. When the barman came to serve me I said I wondered if he'd let me have a glass of water. His face reacted, either to my request or my foreign accent, and he said, 'Why not,' and then brought me the glass of water. Along the bar, but none near me, there were small, sectioned, glass trays with peanuts and crisps. And quite casually, as if more concerned with watching the TV set at the other end of the bar, he picked up one of these trays and placed it beside the glass of water. 'Eat,' he said, still looking at the TV, then walked away. I sipped at the glass of water. I was crying. My shoulders were shaking and I could not stop the sobs that forced their way through my body and out of my eyes. Yet despite my fear that someone would notice me, my most bitter shame and rage was that I had never cried as a child. I could not remember ever having cried as a child. Not to cry was my most potent defiance to those who saw it as their duty, or as the lust of their duty, to make me cry. And now, years later, they had finally won. As they always knew they would. And I knew I was broken for the rest of my life.

A man was standing next to me. He put his hand over mine and left it there. My hunger for food and water was gone and I stared at the food and water in front of me. I had never before in my life felt so great an indifference to anything in my life. Without joy, and with a tight, staring face, I was euphoric. There was nothing left of me now for anyone to hurt or to damage and I had, then, that solace. The man's hand tightened on mine. I saw the scene we presented from the point of view of the eyes that watched from the faces in the bar, and I was neither dismayed nor curious. The man took me to his home. The next morning he gave me fifty dollars and I left New Orleans. When the money started to run low I stopped taking buses and started walking. Where I was going, or why, I didn't even want to know. The money had run out three days ago.

Samuel was still standing and watching my pathetic attempts to rekindle the fire. I stamped on the embers, started to kick and scatter them in a surge of vengeance, and tried, as I always do, to remove all trace of the source of my humiliation. Then I sat down in a defiant sulk and stared at Samuel.

I expected kindness only from a particular kind of man. For the others it was a quality that could never be offered to another man without condescension. It was an act that threatened the independence and masculinity of both the giver and the taker. I had been sure that it must always be so. Yet Samuel, the man who continually re-altered himself in my starved eyes, the man who continually re-altered the co-ordinates of the realities of my world, was relaxed and at peace in the situation between us.

I asked him the time. When he looked at his watch he pressed a button on it and a light glowed from the dial.

'Just after eleven.'

'Thought it was more.' But I was really wondering about the value of such a watch, and how a tramp like Samuel had gotten hold of it.

'So you've really got a house and a farm?'

He nodded.

'And you've got a wife and a daughter there?'

'Sure.'

'And you're going to walk me in at this hour and say, hello, meet a tramp I picked up on the road.' But even as I spoke I realised I was putting the patch of machismo over my brokenness. It was the first time I had ever had the apperception of it, and of masculinity, from this side, and I was conscious that it was comic and childish. It embarrassed me.

'There's nothing to be afraid of, no embarrassment,' he said. 'They'll be looking at TV anyway.'

I dropped the fakery of butchness and laughed. 'Watching TV?'

'What the hell,' he said, 'that's all they do. Why'd'you think I come down here most nights and light a fire, heh? To keep warm?' His head moved, fractionally, and again his eyes were peering into mine. 'Christ,' he said, 'you still don't believe me.'

I imitated the movement of his head and smiled.

'So who's clean and who's lousy?' He shouted, and my smile vanished. 'Who's fed and who's hungry? You keep fooling yourself, boy, and you end up being fooled by everyone you meet. That's smart!'

Again, and by instinct, I wanted to reply with a violence of manner and words, and my body and face were automatically bracing themselves for that. But the stance and the mask no longer fitted. I gave up, and found I was emptied of anger. The man baffled me. I had to accept that now. And that achievement reclassified Samuel in an area of my mind where all of the incomprehensible, the wonderful and the terrifying mysteries of my life, and of life, are sent. It is an area of my mind where all the realities that refuse to be fitted into words are sent.

I felt the influence of the calm that was now in his eyes, and asked as gently and as politely as I could, 'Samuel, I must ask. What's in it for you?'

'What's left in you for anyone?' he asked back immediately.

I sighed and pretended to be hurt. But it was true. There was nothing left of me for myself nor for anyone else. Samuel also exhaled, and sat back down on the ground. I thought he'd given up the ghost.

'I'm an old man,' he said quietly. 'I've worked my ass off to get where I am. I never lived my ass off. I don't know what I missed in life, but I miss it now. I regret missing it.' He looked down at his polished, well-built shoes, and cuffed their toecaps lightly with his fingers. 'I was so busy working like an ant I never had time to look up. Now I've got it made. And I look up. And my life is gone.'

He didn't seem to know, or care, that this fate is not uncommon. I was not moved by the confession. I did not believe the man. I felt for him as if he were a lonely child, abandoned and lost on an empty, still summer afternoon, a child bored by his toys, and waiting for someone to come back home. There was nothing I could do for him. I was not the one he was waiting for to come back home.

Then he laughed. It was a stage laugh, and much too loud and self-mocking. But the aura of venom that exuded from it frightened me. His maniac's laugh continued, then he belched and stopped. I was nonplussed and he saw it. And then the too loud and too despairing laugh recommenced.

I must, to function as a human being, keep a tenuous faith with my judgements as they occur in my mind. But each time I reached a conclusion about Samuel he shattered it a moment later. I was sure he knew what he was doing. And now I was so puzzled by the man I'd have hesitated to deny it if he had told me he was God. When I understood that, I understood the non-normal, the extravagant state of suggestibility that I was in. And all of my faithful suspicions about mankind came back to stand guard inside the small door of my mind. They always do, and they have forever prevented me from forming friendships, from accepting a place in society. At some stage on the road that others pass so easily I am beset by misgivings, by the feeling that I'm being tricked. At that stage I must go down the first turn-off I can find. That is both metaphorical and literal.

Yet I am still tricked, or believe I am. And though I believe I have nothing more to lose, except life itself, I am still afraid of being tricked. Not just of losing, but of being tricked. It is as if this conceit for my life is a strength that preserves me in order, finally, to preserve itself. As if all I ever do serves not me but an ulterior motive of which I must always remain ignorant. So I am left searching for myself in the shambles of my understanding. And all these, all the suspicions, all the turn-offs, all the fears that life as it is perceived is a trick, these are at once the elements and the crucible that turn a person into a wanderer. A wanderer, both metaphorically and literally. They become dreamers. And are bonded by their dreams to wandering.

Samuel's brows were furrowed. His unsettling laugh had long ceased, and he now peered at me through the darkness. I took my gaze and thoughts off him and looked into the quiet and still countryside. I was very near to a depression and a weariness that would make me chance my life just to lie down and sleep. I was beginning not to care a damn, and I knew where I'd had that euphoric feeling before.

'Let's go, Samuel,' I said without looking at him, and stood up.

'Yeah,' he said, again in his kindly tone. Then he stood up, stretched comfortably, and began to stroll away. I followed, knowing I was becoming a part of another man's fantasy. But millions of people do that every day, knowingly and unknowingly. I walked behind Samuel, and my walk took on the manner of a shackled prisoner shuffling behind a prison warden.

We walked in silence. I was concerned with other trivia and paid no attention to time or distance. The weight of my bag started an ache in my right arm. I swung the bag, unthinkingly, over to my left hand and began to pay attention to the surroundings. Then the dogs began barking. It was primitively savage and hate-filled and tore open the peace of the night.

'Ignore the bastards,' Samuel said. Then he shouted: 'SIT!' The howling stopped, and gentle, pathetic whines began. My sensations also had those qualities, but in the reverse order. The fantasy was turning into reality, and in moments I had to radically re-alter my perspective of Samuel. The man was neither a tramp nor a liar nor a dreamer. And I was about to walk into a home that was guarded by dogs, the animals that pestered my life on the road. They have the fanaticism of prison camp guards, and this is the quality that makes me hate and fear them. And this contempt always extends, with greater force, to those who own such animals.

'It's not me,' Samuel said, 'it's Mama. Mama calls them pets.' He laughed, and the maniac's tinge was in it again. 'We really don't know this language,' he said. And I remembered his problem of distinguishing between children and adults. His laughter was almost silent now, and quite normal. There was a slight tinge of nostalgia in it.

The dogs were running by his side and trying to nuzzle

against his hands. We turned off the road and walked towards a large, well-structured house. It looked sedately opulent and calm, and I supposed Samuel drew his placidity and ease from its comforts. From experience I had learned the obvious, that prison puts a caged feeling into a person. It's a feeling that keeps coming back long, long after you're released. I assumed the same forces of circumstances applied to Samuel's nature, yet I already had all the information to know better.

Somewhere on my road, somewhere in New Orleans, someplace before or after, a belief about myself had formed in my mind. I accepted it without thought. It brought relief to my conscious urge to change my conditioned reflexes. I stopped trying to put a brave face on a great shyness, and stopped not feeling nervous or humble in circumstances that dictated those responses in me. I accepted that my conditioned reflexes could never be changed. I was a mere description of what life had taught me to be, but no more. I could never be extrovert, calm, and proud, in circumstances that dictated those responses in the majority of people I had ever known. I had not become what I was taught to be. I had become a description of that failure. So I learned to mask my reflexes. But they would be there always, and only the mask would be under my control. So as naturally as I tried to move my feet and wipe my shoes on a non-existent doormat before I entered Samuel's house, I also braced myself for an ordeal, and set about masking my discomfort.

Every home is a lair of tensions. I feel them as soon as I enter the atmosphere created by the family. I could feel them now and began to blurt about it being a matter of perspective. The dogs were fiends to me and pets to his wife, his offspring children to him and adults to me. Samuel chuckled goodnaturedly, as if he knew I was rapidly organising my defences, and his chuckling provided a needed diversionary action for my efforts. And then I added, 'I think. I'm not sure either.'

'Goddamn,' he said, 'you're never sure of anything, are you.' And we entered the house.

Inside the main door, to the right, a few steps led down to an open-plan kitchen that occupied the entire length of the house. From the room on the left I could hear a TV set, and an old woman's voice called to ask if Samuel was alone.

'You go ahead upstairs and shower,' he said, and pointed to the stairs at the end of the hallway. 'If you don't have a razor use mine.'

I didn't have a razor. I shook my head and propped my bag against the wall. There was nothing in it that I needed to take upstairs.

'I'll fix some food,' Samuel said. 'Go! Wash!' Then he padded into the kitchen, and I walked cautiously along the hall, up the stairs, and found the bathroom. The sight of so much casual cleanness, of so many clean towels lying casually on the warmed rails, brought me so much delight that it almost kindled hope. The only thing I envy the rich is their last meal, or their ready transportation when I'm hungry and waiting for a bus. But once I'm fed and on the bus I envy them nothing. It never occurred to me to consider their rights to their possessions, or to consider their possessions as anything other than their rights. I was afraid of those questions because I sensed that they aroused envy. And envy, to me, is a word that leers from the face of a cretin. So I was trapped by the language that governed my thoughts. I had to, unthinkingly, accept the status quo. And rising to the level of possessions required a quality that was cretinously greedy, selfish and crude. That these qualities, to be successful, also needed determination and intelligence did not alter them. They were not qualities that I wished to have in my character. They were qualities that I tried to banish from my character.

It was an effort that had formed in childhood, and since childhood I had tried to sustain it. It was formed because I had learned that men who read Shakespeare and Goethe, men who understood the highest reaches of science, and who appreciated classical music, were also men who were Europe's most horrific mass murderers.

At an early age I learned the word for the contradiction. It is hermeneutics. It is the deception of defining a man by his attributes, not his essence, his inner, distinctive nature.

Long after I was thoroughly washed I stayed under the steaming shower just to enjoy the delicious water streaming onto my face, over my head, and insensibly massaging my shoulders and back. I was carried away to thoughts of taking such delights for granted. After I had shaved I stepped back into the shower for more delights. Then I had to step out, and dry myself, and step back into my dirty underwear, my dirty socks, my dirty clothes, and to take all of my attributes with me, and all of my masks, including a kindling resentment. It had been like this in the prison in New Orleans. They kept you clean and they fed you. And each day my resentment and hatred for the prison grew. On the door of my cell there was one word: Alien. I laughed the first time I saw it. Three days later I hated that word. But the due process of deporting an illegal alien had to be fulfilled. And day after day, coming back from the canteen or coming back from the shower room, each time I re-entered that cell I felt it attack and try to maul my essence.

The other prisoners joked about nutcases wanting to live in the United States, but they knew nothing of other countries. Besides, that wasn't what I wanted to do. I wanted to live in the world, and I've always been aware that borders are artificial and the essence of an evil discrimination. Most of the other prison inmates had black skins, and all of the guards had white skins, like mine. But it was the word 'alien' on the door that separated me most firmly from the other prisoners. My sense of being stupidly quarantined by the attributes of nationality or skin colour increased. And the rage that engulfed me each time I was put into that cell left me as explosive, and as still, as primed gelignite, standing just inside the door. It took a deliberate effort of will to move, to walk across to the wall at the other side of the cell. Then my resentment exploded and I laid my forehead gently, tenderly, against the wall and pounded the sides of my fists against the wall and choked on my rage. And stared blindly at the wall between my beating fists. How men can live for years in the prison cells I do not understand, unless they stop being men, but display the attributes.

When the tantrum ceased I sat on the bed and rubbed my forehead in the palms of my hands. It didn't matter to anyone but me but via me it mattered to everyone who came into the slightest contact with me. It robbed me of self-pity, and of pity itself, so that I became more and more indifferent to the sufferings of the other prisoners, and to the concerns and happiness of anyone, but my self, but me.

I was moved to another detention centre and lost the privilege of a single prison cell. In the new centre I shared a cell with three other deportees. Deportees were in all the cells, all along the tier, so the tier carried the label 'Aliens'. The next morning I was brought into the warden's office. My finger-prints didn't match any wanted files, but neither did my name match my date of birth at the registry office in Ireland, and at the Irish address I'd given they'd never heard of me. So the warden wanted to know who I was trying to con. It was obvious who I was trying to con. But I pleaded innocence. The warden looked exasperated and bored.

'Please yourself,' he said when I'd finished. 'When they kick you around Shannon don't blame me.' Then he said the Irish didn't take rejects and neither did the US. And that my name didn't sound Irish. 'But that's where you're going. Shannon. Today's flight.' He pressed a button on his desk and moments later a police officer came in.

'That's him,' the warden said and nodded towards me. 'Still calls himself Chaver. Take him away.'

The cop's face never twitched. He hooked me to him on handcuffs and walked me down the corridors and out into the carpark. He opened the lefthand door of a cruise car and pushed me in. I slid across into the passenger's seat. He unhooked the cuff-chain from his belt and got behind the wheel. He didn't try to start the car. He looked abstractly lost in thought, a thought that wouldn't resolve itself into words. Then he said, 'Jesus, I can't do this.'

I looked in the direction of the handcuffs and he automatically reached behind my back and unlocked them. What he said next stabbed at the deepest heart of my prison-induced impassivity, at the compassion I was sure I had left behind in that cell.

'Country's full of coons and they're sending back Irishmen.'

I sat with a bland face. He started the car and drove out onto the streets. What I thought didn't matter, but I experienced the guilt of the great majority who have always stayed silent, in age after age and in country after country.

'Your prints are on file now,' he said. 'No matter where you're picked up, no matter what name you give, it'll be traced to you and you'll get sent down for a stretch. You follow me?'

And I sensed what the idiot was going to do. 'Sure,' I said. 'Sure.'

'I'm Irish too,' he said, 'and proud of it. County Cork.'

'You've lost your accent.' This flatters a lot of Irish people and I said it, to flatter him, as a conditioned response.

'Granddaddy's from County Cork. I ain't never been there yet.' He said this without the slightest taint of sheepishness.

'You'll like it when you do.'

'Is that a fact?' But it wasn't even a rhetorical question. He sounded like he already knew and was being modest about his knowledge.

We'd been driving for about five minutes or more. 'OK,' he said and suddenly swung into the inside lane, jumped the kerb, and stopped. We were about twenty metres from a junction.

'I'm going to investigate a disturbance,' he said. Then he got out of the car, walked across the street, and entered a bar. I was already in a trap, and tripping over one more web wouldn't fret me. I opened the door of the car, got out, closed the door, and walked to the corner. I turned to the right and ran. When I rounded the next corner I stopped running and started to walk. I was penniless. I walked all day and curled up beside garbage cans in an alleyway all night. I walked all the next day. Walked with no place to go, until the desperation turned to barely muted hysteria. And then by accident and in a daze I entered a bar and asked if I might have a glass of water.

The voice of Samuel came through the door. I reached and flushed the toilet, still feeling that I was at once in two worlds. Samuel wanted to know if everything was alright and I had to make a physical effort to re-adjust my mind to the current world. After a moment I shouted yes, and the voicing of the word brought me fully into my present reality. I washed my hands and without cause I realised I was soberly looking into my own eyes in the mirror over the washhand basin. It was easy to see how Samuel anticipated my moods and responses. A child could have looked at that face and read the despondency. I blinked and tried to force a casual blandness onto my face, and it more or less succeeded. But when I looked

away from the mirror for a few moments and then looked
back, I found the same melancholy had re-settled on my
features. I gave up, opened the door and walked downstairs.
At the end of the hall I noticed my plastic bag was not lying
as I had left it. I was sure someone had rummaged in it. It
didn't matter to me, and the thought just passed my mind.

'Mama's gone to bed,' Samuel said and beckoned me down
into the kitchen. There were two plates on the table and
Samuel looked pleased to have performed the service. On one
plate there was a lightly grilled steak and on the other some
breakfast cereal covered with milk. Samuel smiled and pointed
at the steak.

'That's mine,' he said, 'the goddamn cornflakes and milk is
yours.' I didn't mind and sat down to eat. It was very good,
and I took a second helping while Samuel slowly enjoyed his
steak. When I'd finished I sat back, feeling deeply peaceful.

One of the doors in the hallway opened and a heavy,
adolescent tramp of feet stamped down the stairs and into
the kitchen. I thought the total alteration in the atmosphere
would be plain to Samuel, but he carried on as if nothing
unusual was happening. My indifferent attitude had vanished.
I was fully alert. The girl walked past and looked sideways at
me. I kept my eyes on my empty plate, but I knew who had
rummaged through my bag. It wasn't Samuel's style, and
probably not his wife's, but it was certainly in this girl's
manner. Samuel was still chewing with stupid unconcern, and
didn't bother with introductions. The girl opened the icebox,
took out some milk and poured it into a glass. Then she rested
against the closed door of the icebox and stared at me. I
could see no resemblance between her and Samuel, but she
had a weak, unsettled beauty on her face. The pose she was
holding looked unnatural to her but she seemed comfortable
with it.

'So you're the — what did you call him, Pa?' she asked.

'Mr Anon, of course,' said Samuel casually, and still unaware
of the explosive element in the atmosphere.

'No!' she said, petulantly, in the manner of her pose. 'You
used some word from the Old Country.' Samuel's features
twitched for a moment, the oldness vanished from his face,
but only for a moment, and I knew then why an occasional

oddity broke through the Americanism of his speech. An invisible part of me reached out and touched him with sympathy. I was finally beginning to make sense of Samuel. He looked as abashed and also as pleased as a child who had betrayed his own cleverness.

'Na-v-'nad, Sweetheart, Na-v-'nad. It's not from the Old Country. It's from the Old Language.' The girl said hmm, as if she had learned something and understood, and had not exchanged one unknown for another. Then she detonated the atmosphere.

'Looks just like another road bum to me,' she said neutrally. Samuel's face didn't change, but a surge of his anger flooded the room. The girl must have felt it also.

'Ah hell,' she said, and wandered back across the kitchen. But she went out of her path to touch her father's head lightly as she passed, and Samuel's anger was dispelled from the air. At the top of the steps she turned. I couldn't see but I could hear it, and she said, still in character, 'So what's he doing with English books if he don't speak it?' Then the door slammed.

Samuel laughed. I knew that a household language was being spoken between them. I could understand the solitary words, the sounds, but never their household etymology, nor their poise; the household grammar. But my disposition is to assume the worst in such a situation.

'I best go now,' I said.

'We gave up the Old Faith before we came here,' Samuel said, 'Mama and me. So we never bothered with the language.'

'If you can take me past the dogs I'll be alright.'

Samuel looked up at me and began chuckling. 'I told Isa you didn't speak English. That way she wouldn't ask you for any explanations. No embarrassment. I promised you.'

'It's alright.'

'She must have rumbled your bag. You've got books in there?'

'Yes.'

He shook his head, and his open hand rose and gestured and fell back onto the table. It seemed to explain and excuse his daughter's behaviour.

'I love Isa,' he said. 'I go down to the road some nights and

light a fire, just for conversation. Sitting in a bar alone makes
me feel like a tramp.' He laughed. 'How's that for Old Country
talk, hey!' And I supposed he meant Europe. I still hadn't
discovered what he meant by the Old Country. But it wasn't
Ireland. That didn't stop Samuel sharing his humanity with me.

'Want a drink?' he asked. I had never experienced it but I
could understand the claustrophobic loneliness a man might
feel even with the people he loved, the satedness that needed
relief and respite from love. Samuel knew he had me totally
on his side and didn't wait for an answer. He went to a cup-
board at the far end of the kitchen and brought back a small
bottle of whiskey. 'It's an instinct or something in them,' he
said. 'Big male animal like you walks in and they just have to
nose around like cats to see what's up.' We were both laughing. 'Here,' and he handed me a glass of whiskey. Alcohol
had once played havoc with my nerves and I now try to avoid
it. But to please Samuel I raised the glass and pretended to
sip. He sipped appreciatively at the whiskey and set the glass
back on the table. The mere presence of the bottle of whiskey
on the table seemed to relax him.

'Metabolism,' I said, half to explain the girl and half to
staunch any flow of reminiscence.

'Hey!' And this time he seemed startled into an abrupt
reappraisal of me.

'Your father's goddamn seed, Samuel.'

For a moment he stared, amazed. Then he broke into loud,
relaxed laughter and reached for the whiskey. 'I like it goddamn,' he said. 'Goddamn I like it. That's the sort of language
Isa speaks.' He was happy and relaxed and I was pleased to see
him this way. But my mind was occupied with his daughter's
present reaction to our encounter. By now she would know
she had blundered. A road bum? And thoroughly washed and
well-shaved? And her gesture of appeasement to her father,
she hoped I knew, was also a gentle gesture of appeasement
to me. I fully believed the fantasy I was creating.

It is with this vanity that I always react, later, to a social
unpleasantness. I immediately attribute guilt to the others
involved, and believe that they, when alone and reflecting on
the incident, are forced by their own logic to assume an attitude of regret, and see too, the reasonableness of my point of

view. Something in me creates all of this in my mind and makes it all plausible and inevitable. It is very seldom that I realise what my revisionism is doing to me, and very hard, then, to stop it and admit the truth to myself. The truth that the person has probably forgotten the incident, that if they haven't, and could repeat it, their argument would be even more acutely pointed and devastating. I can never believe that hostility and criticism are objective and sincere and untainted by ulterior motives. But of praise I can easily believe it. I know the grossness of this vanity, but it will not allow me to change it. It occurs before I am aware of it.

Samuel banged his glass on the table. 'You're falling asleep again,' he shouted.

'I was thinking about your daughter,' I said before I had time to think, and, realising this, I stupidly smiled.

Samuel softly cleared his throat and raised the glass to his lips. But he stopped the action, and put the glass down again without drinking. I knew what my smile had caused him to think, and I was floundering for a way to turn him off that track.

'She's a lovely girl, Samuel. That's all I was thinking.' I couldn't tell him, in any way that would be quick enough, that I had been thinking she was watching TV and reforming her thoughts to align with my fantasies, but that these were not sexual. I was trapped by the slowness of words.

Samuel reached across the table and took away my glass of whiskey. He was paying no attention to me. 'I forgot, goddamn,' he said, 'she made me forget. Goddamn.' And he seemed irked, not annoyed, and it had nothing to do with me. For a moment I thought he meant that his daughter, his child, had made him forget she was a sexual being, and that I had merely reminded him of it.

'I'm sorry, Samuel. I wasn't thinking of sex. Not at all.' He looked surprised, as if this term that describes the adoration of the womb and the adoration of the phallus, had not been in the terms of his thought. Then he raised my glass of whiskey to his lips and drank the lot. 'That's unlike you,' he said, and smiled, and I wasn't sure what he meant.

I was blundering through the nervous, invisible webs of domesticity, of filial relationships that were too complex and subtle for me to avoid damaging. I know these webs exist, but only by the contortions they produce, by the bewildering and unwarranted reactions to the simplest statements of the outsider. I was caught in the webs now and any way I moved eased one tension and tightened another. I knew I had no objective view of these petted and unpetted animals caged by domesticity. I also knew I had been too long alone, that I could hypnotise myself into any opinion, and still hold fast to that opinion even when the spell was broken. I had to move Samuel's perspective and I had to move mine.

'She is a beautiful young woman, Samuel,' I tried, 'but I know very little about women.' Then I unnecessarily added, 'Like her.'

'Goddamn,' Samuel said, and laughed, and still did not understand. 'I wanted the goddamn cornflakes to open your stomach, then I was going to give you meat. I forgot. She made me forget. Goddamn. You can't drink whiskey on goddamn cornflakes. I knew there was something wrong.' And then he said goddamn again. He was talking in the household language, and I had misunderstood its code of grammar, its metabolism. I had mistaken all of the attributes for the essence in a typical hermeneutic way.

The chair didn't have arms so I had to rest my elbows on the table. This felt inappropriate, but I could arrange myself in no way to sit comfortably on the chair. I had to stand up and walk. Samuel was now preparing the meat. Pacing up and down behind him while he worked would seem an affront.

'I think I'll take a walk outside,' I said.

'Damn dogs will eat you,' he said without turning around. 'You'll make some seed for a lot of pups.'

I laughed and relaxed, but the energy had to come out. I stood up and paced to the far end of the kitchen and back again. My shoulders were hunched and my hands stuck in my pockets. I was at the end of the kitchen on my second run when the door off the hall opened and Samuel's daughter came back in. She didn't look at me and I knew immediately what had happened.

'You ain't eatin' again, Pa?' And I cringed with the realisation that she had listened and overheard every word I'd said. The remark was meant for me, as a ricochet.

'It ain't your goddamn seed,' I said, and passed her by as I paced to the other end of the kitchen.

Samuel howled, almost choking on his laughter. His daughter stood, utterly lost.

'Are you two drunk?' she asked.

'And that's part of me and you, Isa,' he hollered back, bending over.

'What's the hell's goin' on?' she asked, but she was subdued and bewildered.

'Metabolism!' shouted Samuel. 'Goddamn metabolism!' And I had to turn my face away and not laugh so directly at the unfortunate girl as I passed. Yet even in my laughter I had a haunting fear of us as a collective metabolism. It was haunting. Yet it made sense of the worms and the rats eating their way through the superabundance of human flesh buried under the ground all over the world. For that moment I knew the essence of what we were. But I would rather accept the world in our understanding as a conditioned illusion than as a chemical process. Otherwise I would continue, in one form or another and even in parts, as a chemical process for all eternity, for all of what can never end. And whether I had consciousness of it or not, I would exist for that unspeakable length of time. Its duration, the never-ending resurrection of processes that had died to our senses. The last day in every new blade of grass. And it is not the place of a worm or a flower to reason why it was taking place. I stopped pacing.

'He's a real weirdo, Pa, you know that?' Samuel's daughter said. Her eyes were clear and her face untroubled, and I knew she saw the world in perfect definitions of clarity and colour where everything weird and strange had its place in the black borders of madness.

'He ain't accustomed to being round people,' Samuel said, 'and when he is around people, he ain't accustomed to taking them seriously.'

The 'ain't' disturbed my preoccupation with my own bewilderment. It wasn't Samuel's way of speaking and I struggled to recall it and reconcile it to his normal manner of speaking. It brought me back fully to an understanding of their world. I went to the table and sat down. Deliberately I moved my arms from one position to another, here and there, without ever settling. Then I tucked my feet under the chair and folded my arms. The artificiality of the posture could not have been more plain. It was half relaxed and half formal. Samuel laughed, but Isa looked gloomy and slack. I was struggling to make her discard her notions of me, and to let me define myself in her picture of the world. I needed to rattle her notions and assumptions of who and what I was, in the manner of her first posture with her back against the closed icebox door. I didn't believe I could do it verbally, so I aped the artificiality of her pose until she recognised herself, her own aping, in it. She didn't smile. She walked slowly to the table and sat opposite me. Then without any provocation or prompting she very quietly said, 'I know something of the old countries. They never sat down and told me. But sometimes I can feel it around me.'

Her tone and her words pleased me. But there was something wrong. I tried to recall the words, and did so, yet there was something wrong that I could not locate.

'How did you get into the US?' she asked. Her manner was still kind and gentle.

'I jumped a ship in Hueston. I deserted.'

'Goddamn!' she said, and her features alerted themselves in a wave of expectancy. And it was in that wave of alertness that I saw for the first time her resemblance to Samuel. The alertness pluckered and bemused her features in Samuel's exact manner. It was like looking at the face of a young, female Samuel. I smiled and she smiled back. 'The hell you did?'

'Honest.'

'I like it,' she said happily, 'sure as hell I like that. That's really throwing your fate to the wind.' These were words from a popular song, and I wondered if she learned her emotions in the same way. Yet all of the distrust I had imagined she felt for me had seemed to evaporate. Her hair was dark and rich and a strange excitement for her arose in my body.

'You can go to prison for that, you know,' she said in a manner that was Samuel's tramp manner and disconcerted me. I smiled, wondering if she had sensed the excitement that I felt.

'Can't you tell', Samuel asked, 'he's been?' And I started to tell them a cautious version of the story of the cop in New Orleans. It delighted Isa even more, and I could feel an attachment for me forming in her. She seemed to fix all her attention on me, and disrupt her own concerns until she was oblivious of them and of herself. She thought the story romantic and adventurous, and when I told of the hunger, of the blisters that had formed and broken on my feet and then crusted into hard, painful lumps of skin, and told her of the shame and of the fear, she accepted these as artefacts of verisimilitude. But that was all. We were eating good food in secure shelter. These were the artificial, black borders of experience. Humiliation and pain were confused in her mind with discomfort and embarrassment, or with abstractions of these. They were not conceivable to her as realities that broke the best of people and left them with no interest in their fate.

And this Isa thought was rhetoric. Isa was schooled. She named and classified everything in an orderly way. That was the end of understanding. And though it hurt me that this was the limit of her understanding, I still liked her for her unassuming, blithe innocence in it.

Isa, the daughter of Samuel, reformed me in her picture of the world into a character of adolescent adventure, a character who must, one day, grow up suddenly with the value of his experiences, and start going to a steady job every day for the rest of his life. She could not understand that as a wanderer I awoke each day to a day that belonged to me, and that no time of it was pawned as an unredeemable pledge to the pursuit of material survival. I knew the fate that judges us takes seconds, minutes, hours or days, or other timely words, before the moving finger writes.

I accept that life can only be this moment now, and that to trade any passing moment, any moment that may be my last, to my grasping of straws is sacrilege. It betrays me as an hysterical victim. My pursuit of food and shelter must not be differentiated from the process of life by any work that deadens half my waking hours to the experience, for such work does not even distract us from the sound of our coming death. It does not enthrall us. It deludes us into believing that we are not victims, that our grasping is necessary, that our own death is incomprehensible and that we cannot hear it approach.

Isa, daughter of Samuel, danced her life to the sounds of an unseen orchestra. The black borders had no part in it. She was euphoric, for reasons that she did not understand, in the passing of her life.

For a moment I thought she had caught what I was trying to tell her. I thought I saw something alter in her composure. Her eyes flickered towards Samuel's, but he was merrily concerned with his food and concerned to let us talk. She looked back at me with a slight chill on the curiosity of her features, and I thought for a moment she had seen, for the first time, the Cycladic silent face of oblivion staring at her.

It gave me no pleasure to be its midwife and immediately my mind provided me, as it always does, with consolation. For the daughter of Samuel, like all the children of all the Samuels in all their stations of life, are already in oblivion. They madly pursue possessions and the reflections of status. It is their living fate that makes a tragedy of the world, not the hobo's mumbling on a bench with a bottle of wine, nor the addict with the needle, nor the aimless wanderers on the road or the wanderers in science or art, suspicious of the deceptions and deceits of this existence and trying to find their own answers in it.

I told Isa of a town north of Dallas, a city I had avoided re-visiting for sentimental reasons. It was a small town of penny-pinching shopkeepers. In the town I wanted to buy a can of beans, but I had no can opener. So I told the man I'd buy the beans if he'd open the tin for me. Samuel was already laughing, but Isa could sympathise with the shopkeeper's refusal. The shopkeeper told me I could buy a tin opener in the town's hardware store, as if I wasn't aware of this, and missed the point. Or he didn't want to see it. I didn't have enough money to squander any on can openers. So I made do with a rolltop tin of sardines. On the road coming into the town I'd seen a large advertising hoarding. It was illuminated by a bank of tilted arc-lamps, and the ground underneath them was as warm and as comfortable as a bed. I went back there, eased off my shoes, relaxed, and ate the dead bodies of the fishes. Then I slipped into a peaceful sleep. Sometime during the night an automatic throw-switch turned off the lights, and I awoke shivering with the cold. I walked back into the town, put the empty tin outside the shopkeeper's door and walked on.

By now the chill had left Isa's features and she was smiling again, and my revisionist mind had the temptation to think that the story of the resurrection and awakening of the dead is misunderstood.

Samuel was muttering his usual goddamns and shaking his head. 'Goddamn,' he said, 'I wish Mama had stayed up.' He poured out some whiskey, looked at me, then poured a glass for me. 'Mama came to this country with me. She'd understand. A closed tin of American goddamn beans, right in your hands. And the man won't open them. That's a goddamn parable.' He drank his whiskey in a gulp. 'A goddamn parable.'

Isa looked at him quizzically, and then at me, and her look seemed to disown him for insulting her country. The story concerned life, not a country, and Isa had misunderstood. I could understand her bewilderment, but the Judas look disappointed me. It angered me. I looked away from her inquiring, animal eyes. Samuel knew what had occurred and for a moment he looked resigned. It was the look of an old man tired of seeing the young repeat the mistakes of their elders.

Tramping on the roads, and even before that, I had experienced the Judas look, and I knew the head-hanging despair it induces. It is a look that comes from shadows that do not know the particle of eternity in which they now consciously exist. My sympathy for Samuel's resignation increased my anger with his daughter. She was a shadow, a mere reflection of the human being that was Samuel. And it was then that I understood the force and drive for possessions and status as if they were objects of salvation. It is as if shadows are determined to see their substance, a substance of any kind, rather than endure their nothingness. They must hold fast to something, even those parcels of land they collectively call countries and try to find their identities in. They will seek and hold fast to any possessions, even to the grooming of their bodies and their conceits, and in their eyes they are reflected in their possessions and see their status in the universe.

I pushed the glass of whiskey away from me. Samuel took it and poured it back into the bottle. The action surprised Isa, and she looked upset and suddenly displaced from her normal assurance. Her face betrayed it, and sympathy for that fear made my anger leave me. We had, after all, taken her so far into the battle. A few more steps and all the certainties of her life would dissolve in the wilderness of self-discovery. From there she would realise that all our gestures to each other only signal our bewilderment, that we are forever mere handfuls of dust and handfuls of fear. It is too late then to ask whether existence is rational or not. We find our peace and our humility in our mystery, and our reflections and possessions cannot shelter us from our mystery and our awareness that this is all we can ever have, is what we are. There is no room for anything else.

'Are you sleepy?' the girl asked me. Her voice was kind and soft, and a sensation of gladness for her concern touched me. I shook my head. What I felt for Isa was not love, nor pity, but compassion, a compassion I thought my fists had beaten into a wall. That bland apathy could be induced in me, that so much humanity could be taken from me that I cared for nothing but my own skin, and that the processes could be reversed, was of more importance than I could now give to the presence of the girl. Isa spoke into the context of my experience, and there caused a feeling, a sensation, that was vicarious and remote from what she meant. The same sentence, spoken twice, would not twice produce the exact same emotion. And my answer caused a like reaction in the context of her experience. But we could not exchange and also keep our experiences. We were isolated in them, despite our signals, and our signals of speech were a primitive way of sharing feelings and sensations. And this was the signal most often ignored by all of us. We wish to share but we cannot. This is the anguish. And so we panic and send the message of murder to each other. Isa smiled, and whether I was withdrawing deeper into my solitude, withdrawing further even the shadow of my solitude, or whether I had, for the only time in my life, touched the essence of another's island of existence, I did not know.

'What does it mean,' Isa asked, 'what he called you? Nav-'nad?'

'It means a wanderer, or a refugee.' But to me it means much more than that. I remember the refugees, brutally shaken out of their worlds, out of their stations in their worlds, and discovering, in their bewilderment, that they were nothing special in the common universal world. I first heard the Hebrew word na-v-'nad in that context, as I watched a small group of them receive pity and charity. Yet they looked learned and wise, but were huddling together, as if waiting for a storm to pass. Wise is how they looked to me but they were out of place, and sometimes they seemed stilted against the new environment and reacted wrongly to its continuous cues.

This was how I appeared to Isa, and how Samuel had appeared to me. I was continually misinterpreting the cues from the family background and from the American background. I had also put Samuel against that wall of judgement, against the wall of my expectations and experience. To Isa, wanderer and refugee were definitions, labels for unknowns, and they were otherwise devoid of meaning or comprehension.

'But you ain't that,' she said. 'You're just an illegal immigrant.' I smiled and let it pass. Isa was educated, and like so many of the innocents she believed learning was now her servant; she had not learned enough to know that, had she learned at all, she must obey the rules of learning, that science and culture are just the image and likeness of man, and as treacherous, in all their attributes. This was the knowledge I had seen, but not understood, in the eyes of the na-v-'nads.

I noticed Samuel and Isa exchange glances. Samuel seemed irked, as if Isa had embarrassed me again. It was not what Isa had intended. Her face had altered and her eyes were trying to catch ours and to catch the situation, and halt it.

'But gee you only need a sponsor, doesn't he, Pa?' And she spoke much too fast. Her smile glittered for a moment but it was an empty contortion of her features. 'And a job and there's always —'

I banged the table with my fist, stopped, and stared at my clenched fist. Isa paused. Samuel was watching me, half in suspicion and half in apprehension.

'But gee there's lots of jobs if you look. You could make a fortune in towns just cutting lawns.'

'Ah goddamn, Isa,' Samuel shouted. 'Goddamn. He's roamed half the world and you're telling him the answers. You don't even know the goddamn questions.'

I felt the filial webs between them tense and pull, and the intensity of the power that was trapped in those webs. It altered the aspect of both Samuel and Isa, made their faces taut and serious. In embarrassment I looked down at the table. I knew far less than Samuel thought. I did not know the questions. I only had the sadness of being alone inside myself, trapped in my speech-thoughts and in those imageless, wordless thoughts that often made me catch myself staring intently into space, my mind in a state of blankness. Then I would blink and move, and re-adjust to the surroundings that had suddenly re-appeared. Only a feeling of aloneness, of being unable to communicate, in a sweep, to another human being, my thoughts and feelings. To do that, I knew, required the ability, the gift, to love without selfishness. I do not have that gift, and even now, in the company of Samuel and Isa, I felt more alone than ever before.

I heard Samuel, underneath his breath, begin to half-hum, half-whistle, a song I had long forgotten. The name of the song had slipped from my mind, but in its air I sensed again the wet and muddy earth seeped in grey wisps of fog before daylight and the battle-weary soldiers trudging across the torn and bloodied fields. The song was Lilli Marlene, Europe's requiem, or Europe's national anthem, the song all soldiers hummed and whistled across the cursed and broken land of Europe. All soldiers, advancing onwards, marching on to war; to kill each other, face to face or miles apart, in the land of Europe alone where seventy million people were murdered by starvation and the other obscenities of European wars in the thirty-one years between 1914 and 1945. And all these deaths, all these individual seventy million deaths, and all the deaths before and since, make every step you take in Europe a step on someone's grave. And all those deaths were in vain.

One hundred million gallons of human blood, and more than that, seeped into the land of Europe. And still each new blade of grass is green. And there is now more than one orchestra playing, while the encamped ranks of missiles stand at attention. And we, humankind, shuffling or striding, wonder now if our fate depends on the Mendele finger moving, links oder rechts, life or extermination.

And there is no word for this, this rupture between what we are and our attributes, unless this word is humanity in a sense we have never understood before.

And humankind, unable to hear its individual deaths approach, says that so much death is incomprehensible. But to these even their own individual deaths are forever remote, a rupture of existence that will not come this moment. They are not in this universe. They are shadows. Art or science or a novel activity can absorb them, make them cease, for moments, their endless obsessions with their speech-thoughts, make them live and identify with the lives and characters of fiction and shadows. But they stand at the edge of 'a million square miles of terror, stupidity, and barbed wire' and they do not faint, or stand in reverence and bow their heads. They look out at the world, look on the world, and do not see it. They are not mesmerised by the mystery; they are not mesmerised at all. It is not their concern or passion. And they go on, and it is passed on, this survival of the fittest, of the most brutish. This is their doctrine: that the attributes survive.

Samuel's whistling of Lilli Marlene swamped my mind and body with anguish, and with the fear of death. Then a note of the whistling changed, and I could hear the final 'e'. I knew Samuel's Old Country, and why his daughter knew nothing of its ways, and why old age and its vulnerability had not brought Samuel back to his Old Faith. The orchestras play, the missiles stand, and we do not know what is happening. And it will not matter. There will be no survivors to say they did not know it was happening; that it happened so quickly they cannot explain it; that so much death, all the deaths of all the individuals, is incomprehensible. So our last duty is to watch the clock. In this way, we will know the age-long guilt of the great majority of humankind who have always remained silent, who accepted that it was their fate not to reason why.

I looked at Isa and Samuel. Samuel's whistling had ceased, and Isa looked serene, as if the song her father whistled had re-established their rapport and intimacy. Yet I was still obsessed with the wordless thoughts that were a metaphor for existence and the cortège of the living.

When they took me from that cell marked alien and moved me to that detention centre where the tier was labelled alien, I experienced a joy on hearing the voices shout from between the bars. Voices which shouted Spain, Germany, Norway, Yugoslavia, Greece, Italy, and many more. Voices wondering what nationality and predicament I shared. And all of those voices had gladdened my heart. But now, with the memory of hindsight that I always mistake for intelligence, I realised that these shouts were the cries of tribalism, were the savage shouts of head-hunters, of a cannibalism that had attacked and devoured the distinctive, inner nature of each of the members of those tribes. And my primitive chemistry, acting as my master, had responded and blocked out my intellect. Never again. Listening to Samuel's song, but not because of it, a force gathered in me and determined that never again would I be any description of what I had been taught to be. And I am not a concoction of chemical potions wrapped in blood and skin. Not my body, but something else, detains and contains my inner, distinctive essence, an essence I am afraid to call my soul; afraid that all the Old Faiths, and the new, may again pervert its meaning. If I accept that this essence must rule, and leave it to rule with culture and science, then I am greater than the sum of my parts. My blood will flow into the flowing tide, and my essence, elusive and non-enduring, may give with gladness its place in this universe to another essence, that it also may enjoy the fleeting beauty of existence.

It seemed I had always known this. It had merely, now, come to the region of my mind where my human reason and rationality would judge it, but it had come from that guarded area where all the memories and mysteries of existence are stored; the area that is transrational, that must be wary of telling our petty reasoning, of telling our understanding of the world as a conditioned illusion, or of telling our understanding of the world as a chemical process. It must be wary of telling us of all the magic there is in the universe of our minds. It cares for us, and does not wish to make us mad. It blocks out all but what our taught reasoning thinks is reasonable.

An emotional release shook my body, and I laughed. Neither Samuel nor Isa could have understood, but they laughed with me.

'Let's have a drink,' Samuel said. 'We'll get on alright, won't we?' He said it to Isa.

'Sure!' she said, and the tone of relief in her voice was joyous. And I knew then that she had never been able to relax with me, had never felt at ease with me, until her body felt the ease that was sweeping through mine.

We each took a small measure of whiskey. Samuel told me how he had arrived in the US forty-five years ago, and of his struggles to rise in its society. It was these years, his old years, that were more precious and more rich than the years of his youth. The calm, stately house he had built was the sanctuary he had built for these valued years.

Isa and I were the beneficiaries not of Samuel's life, but of the story of Samuel's life. Isa's posture changed as she listened and laughed, asked questions or expressed doubts, and I knew her posture towards life was also altering. My own perspective widened as I listened, and I saw its fleeting place in the universe a little more clearly. I knew of my awareness as he spoke, and I knew, for the first time, why I'd deserted from that ship in Hueston. I could have lived Samuel's life aboard that ship, behaving as we had been taught and were expected to behave. My fretting to leave the ship had come from the trans-rational area of my mind. From that same region came the decision to remain in a New Orleans seaman's bar after a fight had broken out. I didn't run. I carried on drinking. And when the police came and quelled the fighting I knew they'd ask for the shore-passes of the few seamen still in the bar. I had destroyed my shore-pass because it was out of date from the day the ship had left, the day I travelled to New Orleans. When the police asked for my pass I said I had none. I could still have run and I knew it wouldn't bother them if I did. But I sat and faced them. And in the detention centre I was convinced I had been drunk, stupid and irrational.

But only one part of me believed that. Another part of me rejected the I that I had been taught to be; a part that knew that I wanted and needed the experience. It fretted me endlessly into irrational decisions and actions in order to teach me a greater and more comprehensive rationality; a more coherent reality. And though I struggled with words and gestures to explain this to Samuel and Isa they seemed to catch the shadow of the essence I was trying to express, and for odd moments we transcended the metabolism of our existence. It was a feeling we each seemed to know, or sense, an aura from the regions of our minds that refused the slackness of words that are always, and must always be, sounds which never, precisely, convey our intent, precisely, to anyone else. Yet for odd moments our pictures of the world and of our places in it lost their rigidity, became fluid and multidimensional.

Isa, casually, freely, and with ease and grace, talked of the many things that perplexed her, things she never felt comfortable with, things that she tried to keep secret, even from herself. Then she laughed and said she had assumed I was a freeloader on her father's charity, but the simple word na-v-'nad had upset her assumptions and made her inquisitive about me. I smiled and told her of the things my rummaged bag had made me assume about her, and how her posture at the icebox had confirmed my belief that she was a shadow, a description of what others had taught her to be, of what she expected others to expect of her. A woman who existed merely to procreate and who blindly searched for a male to provide the habitat. Isa's laughter roared, and her nature expanded more. She reached across the table and touched my hand. When I told her I had taken her prosperous father for a deranged old tramp hallucinating at the side of a dirt road, the joy of her laughter made her rise and hug her father, and laugh onto his shoulder.

Then I saw Samuel's eyes. I saw them as I had seen them at the side of the dirt road. And I knew why he had used the word na-v-'nad, to me and later to Isa. And the sullen, freezing coldness again swept over me. He had used the word as I had used the words seed and metabolism. Used it to make understanding hesitate, and reconsider. And in Samuel's eyes I now saw that we were, Isa, Samuel and myself, appealing to each other's dreams of ourselves, appealing to our collective dream of ourselves. We were talking to fantasies. We were hallucinating as humans always do, in assumptions of understanding or assumptions of dreams, the assumptions that we believe unite us until chance makes us reconsider and we discover that they always divide us.

My numbness spread and Isa's happiness hesitated and began to fade. I was afraid she thought I had tricked her and tried to speak. I spoke but there was no fluid response. Isa retreated from her re-altered picture of me, and retreated from her trust in any of her pictures of the world. And perhaps she sensed, then, that we were, all of us in this world, unknowable to each other.

Samuel stood up and collected the glasses. He said he'd show me my room. We said quiet, cautious goodnights. I entered the room, undressed, went to bed, and lay awake for hours, my mind wondering and absorbed by the aleatory randomness of my life, and its strange results. Results that were no more understandable to my reason than the science of sub-atomic physics and the indeterminacy of identical particles in their inter-action. And I thought the word Samuel used to describe me described it all. Na-v-'nad, restless wanderer and fugitive, obeying the transrational impulses of a consciousness that was beyond conscious reasoning. The reasoning consciousness made rules, advanced, and then broke the rules it had used to advance, formed new rules and blithely advanced again.

It seemed that only moments later Samuel was shaking me awake. It was ten o'clock in the morning. I took a shower, and came down to breakfast. Then I met Mama, and she sensed immediately my anxiety at treading through the domestic webs. She said Isa had gone to visit friends and would be away all day. I went to sit at the table and Mama came behind to seat me, as casually as if I were always treated this way. Then she cuffed my hair back and forth, and laughed, and smoothed my hair back into place with her hands and softly laid the open palm of her hand on the nape of my neck. It was the most beautiful sensation I had ever felt, and all my fretfulness was dispelled. I felt that this old woman had known me for years. And for breakfast, instead of cereals and milk, Mama cooked a steak for me. Then we said goodbye, and Samuel drove me to the nearest town.

Samuel knew the road I was on and didn't bother to offer me a job, or to find me work, or to ask if I needed money. He laughed when he handed me the rover's bus ticket, valid for three days, and slipped the money in between the books in my bag.

It made no difference. Two weeks later I was broke and hungry and near despair, and by accident and in a daze I entered a bar and asked if I might have a glass of water. The barman said why not, and brought me the water. Five minutes later a police officer entered the bar, walked straight to me, and asked for my identification. Leaving the bar I noticed the barman whistling as he polished the glasses.

In the police station I deliberately ignored my surroundings and ignored the uniforms on the men who questioned me. I told them everything and used that as a defence against the surroundings and the uniforms, and used it too as an escape against my feeling of being trapped, trapped for a length of time that I knew my mind would not be able to bear. The next day I learned that no imprisonment awaited me, and the day after that I arrived in Shannon.

A police officer met me at the airport. He was old and very cautious and eyed me quizzically, unsure of what to expect. I smiled and said it felt nice to be home again.

'Indeed,' he said relaxing. 'And how did you like your trip?' A baffled understanding startled across my face.

'My God in this dark muffled night you mustn't play God anymore. The world is a die already nicked and rounded from too much rolling by chance, and must come to rest in a hollow place in the hollow of its enormous grave.'

Vallejo

STOLEN AIR

'I'LL BE SHOT at dawn this morning,' he answered her.

And she — her eyes skimmed the aperçu and she — she nimbly hesitated. Then she laughed.

Alone, he watched over his mind and remembered nothing of the remainder of the night. Nearby, from the river Thames, a ship's whistle abruptly roared its hoarseness across the darkness of the prodded, reluctant water. Later, before the sudden loneliness of a new day, the spired oath of a church bell struck against the peace of the morning. Later still came the solace from the gently rising noise of an awakening city, of trucks easing the roar of their engines along the dock road, the sudden, broken, clang of noise from the shunting yards, the aired release of power, of a solitary train then commencing to growl, the caught gasp of its power, and its then contented rut along the open railway tracks. Another drift of time unmarked by noise, before the gulls began to caw and shriek. And soon the morning was fully born.

The past attained no sense of fallen distance. It was not away. It moved concurrently to the present as a wave broadens its crest further along the rush of its advance. It now uncovered the cleft where the Watchman's existence concealed itself. He felt the touch, the awakening response, the concentration and concurrence of expression to the anxieties of inner life. A renewed stammer of life, unkempt with doubt and guile, self-subterfuge, and moments of groomed honesty, with moments, also, that were chasmic and without self-guile, of glimpses raised across the steppes of uncharted consciousness, of awareness reined tightly in against the fear, the self-enquiry silent, nervous, alerted to its own silent demand for an echo. And still the silence of the steppes, answering not at all to any probe nor sweep of metaphor. Without the paths, the ribbons, the solid traces of language gone before, the unaroused words unquitened themselves, turbulently reared, shied, moved accidentally forward in a stumbled panic, stumbled onto the verge of untrodden emptiness and thrust, again and again, thrust the reared, naked belly of their substance into the surrounding strangeness. Words were again alive, and again as active as the turbulent cries of the rising gulls.

Few wanted the job. It asked for the most silent hours of the night and morning, from 9 p.m. to 7 a.m., the hours when solitude and self-communion might briefly visit a mind, might steal from the silence a solace to nourish a mind against the deadening, over-crowded, noise of a city torn into over-crowded, broken houses of flats and bedsitters. And relentlessly pierced into these for the first time was the flowing excitement of the first transistor radios, the first constancy of onanism from the radio voices, and the placid, encompassing, jumped and stamping power of television. Against these, this commonality in the London of '67, walls and doors created no more privacy than railed curtains. Few wanted the job of patrolling this ancient building where the women and children were housed. And occasionally their men, too. But always very few of their men. And each was the solitary cortège, most often the floundering, boisterous wake, of a life redundant of itself.

In the innermost slump of forgotten hopelessness, the place beyond any doubt, each was inert to the nimbling risk, the agility of response, that directly echoes the nervous throb of existence. There was in each an untouched bewilderedness, a bewilderedness to the risk, to the fluid, treacherous exuberance, to the pulse, the handled feel, of anxious joy alerted by the probe of individual, self-conscious inquiry. It was all incomprehensible to them. And they were then fully conformed to the pattern of society, clearly cut for a limited purpose, their concerns fully cloned. But they had fought no battles with realities, and were never defeated, never aware of being prisoners of life, and never so much disturbed by the presence of their life as they were by thoughts of its death.

It was the Watchman's first night of patrolling the corridors of the ancient building. Below at the main door there were uniformed security guards. Their attitudes were demonstratively impressive. They were so by imitated and immense effort, and their slowed deportment was eased and satisfied with a conscious, imitated pride. There was little about the inhabitants of the House that they hadn't seen too often, little about life at all that surprised them, little that they, and experience, hadn't kinda figured out for themselves, like everyone else with brains. Then they moseyied on over for a fresh beaker of water.

The Watchman returned upstairs. And this time he accepted when a woman from one of the cubicles offered him a cup of tea. In slippers and dressing-gown she settled back to watch the television, and said that she always got to know the watchmen. None of them lasted long, but they were safe and ready company. Then she flicked the ash from her cigarette. It was nice that the watchmen didn't have the prison-warden attitude of the security guards, she said, having said it many times, and snugly sure that it flattered. The Watchman sighed, and wondered why he shouldn't be safe company with such a knackered woman. The woman noticed the change and looked at him. The Watchman looked away. In the corner of the room, against the brightness of the light and the blare of the television, a child was sleeping. The woman said the child was used to it. And in her voice again was the casual and forgotten certainty that the child's condition was thereby made normal and legitimate. And an assurance, too, that the child could not know its situation was questionable, could not know that its situation was open to challenge, that the givenness of its placed condition was wrong. No child ever does. It may be curious about its universe, but it cannot be subversive of it.

And the Watchman, still vague in his roaming suspicions that the nature-given state of life was questionable, had no addressable target for the doubts that groped and probed wordlessly about his mind and there made renewed acquaintance with the congealed past of experienced reality, glimpsed unworded memories, and wondered to itself. And contentedly his mind mulled about so as he paced the corridors. The hours passed. The cabins along all four floors of the building became silent. Occasionally the steel grill of the ancient elevator painfully sounded as it was pushed open or closed. Then silence, again. And the warmth of the security again alive in his mind that he had found a job immediately on the day of his arrival in London.

Morning, and the end of the first shift, arrived in a blinked perception of so many hours suddenly gone. Freed, then, from the onus of his passive work, the Watchman left the building and walked home to the Seamen's Rest. When he awoke it was evening, and he awoke gently in a long-sought contentment, that with thrift and endurance, with slyly placed discreetness, silence, and with watchfulness, independence of the need for these things would again return to his life and activities.

And in an ease of fear the days began to quietly and rapidly pass. The Watchman withdrew behind the facade of his work. Weeks passed, and he remained a stranger to the inhabitants of the House. He knew of them, this ragtag section of the barrio-poor of London, those cast-off and pregnant, unmarried women, the unmarried mothers, the smaller number of families evicted by landlords, the smaller number of families left homeless by fire, and of the large number of battered, abandoned, or runaway women who had left their homes. Left, in the manner of fleeing, from the natural or drunken violence of their once chosen men. They all waited now in the care of the Borough Councils of London, waited for the Councils to provide family accommodation, and did so in the unexamining and quaint manner in which they also waited for their lives to pass, ever ready and innocent to believe that all their hopes were imminent of unexpected, wild fulfilment. Their empty days were replaced by empty days. And they did not notice.

They lied, they exaggerated, and by gesture and attitude did everything possible to masquerade and edify their condition. This facade, this process of edification, had become the purpose of their lives. And somehow, without going mad, they concealed from themselves their own lies. And by this each judged the success of their human existence. All succeeded; none rebelled against themselves; and all had winter in their faces and a fallen lack of human grace in their stilted manners.

The House had its own larval smell. It was the essence, the inner, most exact definition of the building. It absorbed and was spiritually changed by the individual and the mobbed activities of all the homeless people that it housed. And the change was larvally slow, minute, and determinately solid. Once military seamen had lived in these ancient barracks of rooms. The charged, negative energy of waiting, of abiding in an emptiness of time, an edginess that seeped into the House, became its ebbing life, its answering presence and echo, its entire ontology —. — And the oddity of the unsought word, the unexpected contact of its probe, grounded the Watchman's concerns. The building reverted to its visible and audible presence. It was dirty and old. Its noise had the wavering resilience of a hallucination that the mind's eye clearly saw from a mind that refused to accept the reality, the separate life of the hallucination, refused to focus on it, and found it still resilient everywhere it turned.

The pale nightlights, soft and soothing, lost their effect against the glare of the main lights along the corridors. Again and again, throughout the nights, the Watchman had merely to switch off these brazen, disquieting lights as he endlessly walked his rounds in a cautious alertness for any signs of fire. Bored and ignored children raced past, women repeatedly came out to complain, shouted and screamed their enraged demands for a bit of peace; and the children then mocked and screamed back the adult threats that childish spite now magnified into adult obscenities. Locales of stung rage were created, rage that was vocal but inarticulate, phatic, and immediately and hissingly poisonous to thought and reason. Radios and TVs increased their powered volumes, and competing solitudes of deafening noise raged against each other from cabin to cabin. Again and again. And again adults and

children noisily disrupted adult and childish noise. And again.
And an insanity, the primeval, corrosive insanity of a persistent
and persistently disguised hysteria emerged and grew into the
physical, moving life of the building, and became the mentally
paralysing, nervous mould of all of its inhabitants.

On such a night a short, squat man, tattooed on both arms,
approached. He was jolly in his approach, smiled, and said
he'd heard the Watchman was also an ex-sailor. The man spoke
in a manner buoyant with corblimey chumminess. Yet there
was the tough impress of an experienced seaman in his manner,
and his eyes dimmed in reaction to the Watchman's lack of
instant response. The Watchman saw a common loneliness in
the jolly man's eyes, a burnt offering of understanding the
other's past, of strangers whose immediate points of contact
and reference are common in outline, and whose inner patterns
have no concurrence. The Watchman's head nodded. The jolly
man smiled again. He pointed at his arms and said the Watchman would never have gotten the job if he'd had tattoos, that
the bleeding social worker thought all sailors without tattoos
were bleeding queers. The jolly man, the ex-floating, insular,
parochial ship-villager, the clown, never stopped saying bleeding. It conditioned and balanced every sentence he spoke. And
each new sentence emerged from a deeply etched, deep-
structured, imitative yet uniquely juggled, regenerative matrix
of cliches. The Watchman smiled back and said he'd whistle
Lilli Marlene on his rounds. The jolly man laughed.

'Bleeding great that,' he said.

At the job interview the woman had watched his movements
as he entered the room. More objective of the Watchman's
mannerisms than her own, her movements and her formation
of questions portrayed an image of the applicant she wanted.
And with accidentally disclosed effeteness the Watchman
reformed his responses to that image. Or almost so. It wasn't
difficult, not for a young man already gutted of confidence.
His application was earnest by circumstance. He was no
natural threat to women. And he spoke in a quiet and handy
way of changing fuses, clearing sumps, of being handy with
such rough and ready household jobs whose awkwardness
rasped against the patience of women.

It was bleeding great, the jolly man said again, cos everyone

knew queers couldn't whistle. And the jolly man's evergreen
wit held itself ready to guffaw at the trick for the umpteenth
time. Then his face looked confused, then cheated, then stared
silently at the bewonderment on the Watchman's face.

The jolly man, the man anxious of all outlines, said he
needed a chum's favour. He wasn't like the rest of the bleeding
layabouts in the place. He and his missus worked, until the
baby came —

— And there the Watchman unexpectedly raised the opening fists of his hands and stopped the man's speech. He asked
what the jolly man wanted. The jolly man laughed, relieved,
the sudden roughness of the Watchman's manner a needed
reassurance against the still undetonated joke. And a rapid
chumminess ensued. At its end, stripped, almost, of corblimey
chumminess and true-as-jesus cliches, it meant that the corridor
children left the steel grill of the elevator open, deliberately,
and so the jolly man's wife, to heat the baby's bottle, cos
they hadn't bought an electric kettle yet, had to walk down,
and back up from the communal kitchen, four flights of
bleeding stairs for the 6 a.m. feeding.

In the Watchman's concerns an area of self-protective mist
silently moved. An inner translation, a crossword, a guessed-at
context, abstracted the intended meaning from the jolly man's
speech. The Watchman was newly and dimly conscious of it,
and wondered about himself. From their common words a
reciprocal meaning was missing. It was much more than the jargon that they spoke a different kind of language, that the slant
and shaft of language, the thrust of words from the common
motherlode of language was forever of an accidental uniqueness, that between these thrusts conduits of understanding
were wrongly assumed, and labyrinths of cross-understanding
endlessly created.

It wasn't even a class difference of outer speech and of
inner, class-exclusive, coded meaning. Nor a difference of
range and vocabulary, but one of probe, trace, and wordless
scanning, not for fitting, gloved words, but for touched,
handled meaning, the identity of thought in the bounded and
porous, the spurred ontology in the life of each word, and its
striking power to energize an image, or a hallucination of an
image, into a clear and resilient, wavering reality, alone, pre-

cisely true, and replete of the activity of thought. And language, then, the meaning and life of its words, was something more than a regenerative and phenomenal consensus.

Silent mists formed by months of dutiful work slackened in the Watchman's mind. His willed endurance to work in the House was coming to its own end. He promised the jolly man he'd bring the elevator to the fourth floor at a quarter to six each morning, and leave the grill gate open. The missus could close it herself, descend, leave the grill open —

'— Bleeding great that, bleeding great,' said the jolly man, and the Watchman passed by and walked on. 'Ta,' said the jolly man in chummy thankfulness. 'Tat-ta.' And the Watchman's footsteps hesitated on the beat of the words.

He walked on. The protective mist of silence and endurance evaporated. He longed for an end to the overcrowded press of empty solitude in his life, longed for contact and communication with life's essence.

He walked on. Soon, the midnight hours descended and silence lay across the night. It was a silence without softness, a hurried, hushed noiselessness. Somewhere there was a sound. He turned and heard it end. The steel grill of the elevator was pushed open, but not closed. And a very young woman walked sprightly into the corridor.

'Can't you close a door on a lift,' he demanded.

'Fuck off,' she said with instant American casualness, and hesitated, and all of her youngness, all of the mellow, untried lust in her girlish eyes swept reluctantly over him. She blinked her eyes, and raised a hand to the side of her face. Disobediently, the Watchman ignored her and walked past. He entered the elevator and closed the gate. The elevator slowly rose, rose much too slowly. At the fourth floor he slid the gate open, left it so, walked along the softly lighted corridor, lifted the brace on the fire-exit door, kicked the goddamn, sticking, fucking thing open, stepped out onto the fire escape, and climbed the stairs to the roof.

The night's sky was just another night's sky. It was ineffably beautiful, Gedali, wayward and numbingly beautiful. The light was turned on in the moon. In the depths of the universe there were stars all in stipple. They were free, and millions of safe miles from this tiny rock of Earth hurling purposelessly

through space. He watched the beauty of eternal silence, its
open, sublimal paradise. A final nerve screamed within, and
the net of morale, the net of culture, of its specific condition-
ing, lost its moulding pull on him. The narrowness of intent,
of enduring to endure, of struggling on to arrive at some
understanding, some mental oasis of understanding and recon-
ciliation with reality, the reality to him of his life and death,
had passed away. The ethos of the people in the House, people
everywhere, the sustenance they fed their minds, their sense
of purpose, the psychology of private and collective morale,
the pheromone they suckled from the ethos around them,
the pheromones of social, religious, political, professional life,
cloud and mystify the awesome steppes of uncharted consciousness in the universe, and in their minds, and gathers
strength to believe in personal salvation against the barrenness
of the constant mass spasms of lives existing between oblivion
and oblivion.

The Watchman looked down at the yellow street light far
below him. To have come so far for this. Almost twenty
years of growing that had passed as rapidly as the next twenty
years must also pass. A forced march from birth to grave, learning the names of the perennial flowers. A blinked, unfocussed
consciousness as the hole in the ground rushed towards him,
or the challenge to rush now towards the pushed placidity of
the inevitable, to the forced acceptance of death.

The sheer drop of the fall terrified him. He walked backwards from the edge of the roof. There was no sensation of
relief, of a life of struggling-by, making-out, a life of getting-
by, no sense of life regained from the loitering certainty of
death. Fear, above all else, fear bound him to life, and made
its own comment, that life is a cursed, a mistaken, a worthless
trial. Only a God in our own image, petty, primitive, and
unjust, would place us in this prison of existence.

To have endured, desperate and silent, all these months,
from the pre-dawn landscape of Shannon Airport, to have
been a deportee and re-introduced, penniless, and nervously
broken, to Ireland, the native country, a country with an
agelong tradition of defeat, repression, rebellion, and terror.
And all this was its glory, and the source of its memories, its
passions, its future; its sense of keen uniqueness and exception

among the common run of nations. Bewildering oddities of gesture and response everywhere confronted him. And most obviously he appeared too deliberately foreign to his one-time countrymen. Locally urbane, measured exasperation passed for tolerance in the barter of all exchanges. And his ready willingness to concede his unhoused foreignness was matched by no understanding that the local intercourse of accents and gesture were elsewhere, everywhere else in the world, as stunningly strange, foreign, and as exasperatingly affected as his. The strength of the forelock'd parochialism, of its brutally assumed sense of the righteousness of its humbug, was numbing. And it was this, the narrow, penned inability, the reared and cultured refusal to comprehend the equality of strangeness, that made his mind retreat to internal exile. In no eye, voice, or gesture was there a given understanding that they were all equal and temporary guests of existence, that death patiently awaited each, and never responded in any way to their spiritual superstitions of salvation. Caretakers of themselves without tenure in this existence, they abided by belief in another existence, and religiously avoided the vertigo of the experience of Being. Self-conviction was firm on their faces. They were owners of property, holders of jobs, disciples of eternal beliefs, and all was accounted for. And thus embalmed they passed away their lives.

Loose-footed beliefs never gained so much ground, never knew such contentment. And on the walk along the road the fear pitted itself in his stomach that this was the loneliness of native foreignness in every country on this tiny planet, the live, charged state of being propertyless, jobless, and forever hearing in all beliefs tested against experience the plain, common ring of hollowness. This was home. After the open seas, after hoboing in the Americas, this was home. Within the hour it had again the claustrophobic familiarity of a prison cell. And onwards, in deepening silence, in the hitch-hiked journey to Dublin, that forever open sore of unemployment. Dublin, and the pudenda broad and squat accents of so many of its women, the frightened, sharp uneasiness of so many of its men, the nervously prostrate and limping emotions of manic sexual repression and frustration scalding visible everywhere in this city of hospitals and churches and the pious adoration of perpetual tragedy, of rites performed in time to genuine grief, the theatre and remission of stilted, embalmed lives.

It is a bereaved city, a de-energised city, a city continually gutted by the emigration of the major portion of its native talent and enthusiasm. Stray dogs shamble everywhere about its abused streets and the sense of an aftermath, of uncared for desolation, is complete. The barrio-poor from the dole· queues, and those in the queues above, tread their apologetic way amid the sly greed and unctuous banditry of the getting-on, and the much more than middle, bandit class. They dislike their very own ilk, and hate, utterly hate, everyone else.

Like so many others he railed, inwardly and helplessly, his spirits floundered, and he left.

Gedali, whatever your fate, you would understand this loneliness, this wounded outpouring. It is when there is nothing left but fanatical hope.

'HEY!' she called, and sounded barely controlled, frightened, and very American, '— You looking for smut here too!'

He turned towards her. She again raised a hand to the side of her face. Again he recognised the bashful, vulnerable lust in her unsettled, girlish eyes. And all of it was deliberate. And most innocent. But the preliminaries to having her, the faked quantities of concern, interest, affection, passion, waited indefinitely before him.

'Tat-ta,' he said.

And she — her eyes became bewildered, looked lost, and the young wisdom in her eyes looked askance at the oddity of the commonplace. Her eyelids flickered, and deliberately her features moved into a testing half-smile. Then all collapsed tragically into solemnness. It was superb, Gedali. She stood there so humbly proud, and freshly proud of that, and so solid against all the vagaries of fortune, convinced that the greatest of ill-storms must finally ebb against the will of her youthfulness. Then she spoke like a child, with a penitent's aura about her subdued voice, the aura of long-alone guilt and doubt, as if in this manner she must begin, and told what the knackered, used women in the House said about the Watch-man, of her being alone and joining in for companionship, of enjoying at first the warm, doggish enchantment, the European discontent with everything except their individual selves; quite pleased, rather, with their individual selves, their placid, still-water, fetid contentment with their selves, the stupid old bitches, until they were really fucking irksome to be with, she said. They had nothing of their own, not really, no self-generated beliefs, or questions, or character. But they had all these things as hand-me-downs, with comfortable alterations here and there, and even the goddamn alterations were copied; strange bits and pieces from characters in the soap-operas mixed up with the gossip lives of the actors. It took time to see through them, then suddenly they were so goddamn hollow and boring. Their boredom jagged itself into all her thoughts. Her real solitude of herself was invaded and occupied. They overcrowded her and took over her solitude, and it was loneliness then; real, overcrowded loneliness. And it was fucking agony.

'Hell I just had to snap at somebody,' she said, 'I'm sorry.'

'Come and I'll show you a great wall.'

'A great wall?'

'If you ever want to talk to a wall it's a great wall.'

Innocence, anxious and rapacious innocence, and the flipped desire for the gypsy experiences of adolescence, came quickly alive in her smiling eyes. He took her into his arms. She nervously laughed a little. But the soft willingness to be embraced, to take the caress, to be gently and firmly wanted, but not to be used, waited and watched in the slight turn away of her shoulders, about the timidity and fear of rejection in her still unsure, young adult eyes. He whispered his vulnerability to her, told her a little of his time at sea, his hoboing in the Americas, his penniless deportation back to Ireland and his flooded relief to have found, when he made it to London, this miserable job of night Watchman in this place for home-less people, and his numbed surprise that almost all of these people were battered wives, abandoned wives, runaway wives, unmarried mothers, and thrown out pregnant daughters. He had never known so many broken and knackered women existed. Then he whispered many lies and many truths, and she giggled, neutrally. He told her of the past of many experiences now congealed into the present, and of the nervous solitude of these memories. She whispered that she hated the past and wanted it to be forever gone, hated her fled American father, her English mother, the vicious, drunken rows, and the memories of childhood were still too raw to be touched, even re-touched, by consideration and thought. She pressed herself against him, and hugged him. A moment later he was aware of time gone and of her silence, her contented, relaxed silence. She moved her body against him. The tensile strength of her body ached against him, and moved, and ached again. She ached superbly. It was consumate, of her nature, her natural learning, of her nubile instinct of herself, her svelte, unhurried joy of desire, its lick on her skin, the probing new taste of sexual freshness intoxicating her, and her open, aching joy of desire. She moved, slightly, half-steppingly, one leg closer against him, and the palms of her hands relaxed and regained their pressure on the small of his back. There was a breathed silence and everywhere the taste and smell of skin. She pulled herself back and for moments she looked plainly and unsmilingly at him. Then she tightly settled back into their embrace.

'Christ,' he said.

'I don't mind,' she answered.

They went below, walked in a drifting absent-minded way through the stilled peace of the corridor, and were everyway alert to the coming rendezvous of their bodies.

'She sleeps across there,' she said, tilting her head backwards towards the door of the opposite cubicle.

'Who?'

'My drunken English Mommy,' she said, and each word was empty of emotion. There wasn't even exasperation in her voice, but a placidness, a heavy placidness far beyond any stirring of concern.

She closed the door of the cubicle behind him. There was at once an abyss of silence, of suddenly too many possibilities of gesture, too bloodthirsty a craving now stumbling and bucking under its own force, now jumping out of measure with any word, any gesture, while their eyes tried to avoid each other's growing nakedness, then each became the other's supplicant, and the other's hungry foe, as they eased and forced their bodies into the chaos of sex. There was for him the squeezed, stretched joy of relief on entering in upon her body, an almost instant, warm relief on the threshold of entry.

At the last moment her held breath whispered that she was a virgin; the exact word, and the deepest probe of magic to his instincts. A silent moment later, without ado, her held breath eased itself.

'Thrust,' she said.

His instincts and his body leaped. And there was then a fervour of lust and ecstasy.

In a remission of warm relief, in a concern to save her from any feeling of mere hurried use, he told her she was the transport and entrance to paradise. She giggled comfortably, was otherwise not surprised, and moved to let him more amply nibble on the budding ripeness of her schoolgirlish breasts. They were stippled moulds of beauty and glistened with the moist freshness of apples in Eden. She giggled again, as deeply and as comfortably as before. There was not even an inhibition of conceit in her released attitude of happiness and affection. She lay like a young queen of the earth, and lightly bore all the joys she carried in herself for gods and men. She paid no heed to him. Her still-entered body became alert again and began to move. Her body trembled. All of her body trembled. The tighter he held her, the more he strove, the more her brave body trembled, trembled as if instilled and hurt by a demon that she alone could not exorcise. All of her most nakedly trembled, and the features of her face were held aside and limp with shook endurance. Yet more she trembled. Then she unsettled all, and blessed all; then she whispered: 'Thrust harder.'

A pandemonium of noise intruded through the upper layer of sleep. It was an unembodied noise, distant, of only alien pertinency, and fitted not at all any immediate pattern of memory or anticipation. And sleep still muffled the rappings on the door. It was a nuisance, but otherwise had no relevance. The Watchman turned back towards the healthy depths of sleep. There was more noise, a woman shouted, men shouted, the girl beside him spoke in anxiety and panic and slid quickly from the bed. The door of the cubicle opened before she reached it and the Watchman sat up nakedly awake.

'Cor blimey,' said one of the security guards. The girl turned and grabbed a sheet from the bed.

'Like bleeding animals,' said the other, gaping security guard, and was pushed forward into the room.

'There she is the slut,' said a knackered-faced woman.

'You fat old cow,' said her daughter. And the staggered security guard's outstretched arms barred the woman's outraged approach.

'Get out,' screamed the girl. 'All of you. Get out.' She screamed it again.

'You were never any bleedin' good,' her mother said. And the security guards moved backwards towards the door.

'Later,' said one. 'Later. And the social worker is gonna want to see you,' he said to the Watchman.

'Fuck you and her,' said the Watchman, depressed of any serious emotion.

'The mother says the girl's under age,' the man shouted, and a stung rage itched and sweated instantly about his face and manner.

'Fuck you all,' screamed the girl in despair, 'fuck you all,' and rushed to the door. She pushed it to, and snapped down the latch on the lock. 'Jesus,' she said with despair and relief, and walked slowly back to the side of the bed. She looked thoughtfully at the Watchman, smiled, and sat down gently on the edge of the bed. And once more the bed groaned softly its traitorous, creaked lament against the listening silence of the House.

'What are we going to do now?' she asked.

'I'll be shot at dawn this morning,' he answered her.

And she — her eyes skimmed the aperçu and she — she nimbly hesitated. Then she laughed.

'I have to go, you know,' she said. 'but not there,' and glanced at the washhand basin. 'They all do, goddamn them. Will you see me down the hall?'

He dressed rapidly. She slipped on only her dress. In the hall the mother's listening vigil broke into obscenities. The girl moved silently alongside the wall, the Watchman beside her.

'I'll fucking murder her,' the mother screamed, 'I'll fucking-well murder her.'

'Go away,' the Watchman shouted, and angrily heard fear in his own voice.

'You fuck off,' she screamed into his face. 'You'll get yours.'

'Go away,' he shouted again, and again the nervousness in his voice, and its stinking pheromone, betrayed him. And the woman's coarse, triumphant laughter leered into his face.

'You!' she mocked in her sweet, lout's bravery, 'ya fucker, you hit a woman! That's all you'd be bleedin' good for.'

His fist hit her hard and twice across the face. She fell to her knees and droplets of blood came from her nose and lips.

'Ya fucker,' she roared, and spat blood, 'ya bleedin' fucker,' then she crawled and rose and scurried off down the corridor.

The girl looked on indifferently. 'Wait,' she said. Moments later she came out of the bathroom. She named a time and a place where the Watchman could later meet her, then left him to kick open a rear firedoor and walk free onto the street long before the arrival of the security guards.

At the Seamen's Mission he unscrewed the electric light-switch in his room, deftly withdrew his savings from behind the live wires, then settled down to wait for the morning to be fully born. There was a recuperative weave in the pattern of his nerves. He felt bouncy, free spirited, and eager to command the direction of his life. He was sexually assuaged, and he was proud that his unadmitted desire for a virgin had been so keenly fulfilled. And he was proud also of his masculinity, healthily proud of the masculinity that had satisfied the fresh love of a young woman. He was proud of that, and of the feline health it gave to his nerves.

Outside in the street those normal people, the survivors, the progeny of the fittest and their favorities, were busily starting their casual, daily activities.

Overhead, he heard the lovely caw-caw of a late rising gull. And its soaring flight and cry touched the milieu of his heart.

'Or am I really dead, and are you just experimenting with my soul?'

Go Ask Alice, Anon.

ULOSIS

WALKING TOWARDS HIM up the street she looked bashful, smilingly bashful, and obedient. Steps away she shouted, 'Hi!' then arrived, intentionless, before him. His nerves coiled at the raw closeness of her sexuality; her young-legged, blooding sexuality. He could everywhere smell his own appetite, and hers. And he, the starved, craving, desperate male, saw prey, ripe and fresh, and curiously alerted and attentive, on the svelt of his gaze. Then he could no longer look. Sensations, memories, knowledge, longings, the taste of running blood in his mouth, the fear of another's sexuality so newly alive, close, and hungry in its courtship, tensed and suppressed the kindled responses within him. Her querying eyes still waited. He bent himself to move his head towards the face that blossomed and smiled like a flower as he crossed an infinity of feeling to kiss her open mouth. 'Hi,' she said again, and quietly, as if to ease his movement through the resisting space.

So like a sonnet, a ripening sonnet, so lucidly alerted to the developing power and newness of her feelings, to the embodied resonance of flesh, of romance, of lust, of prolonged, aching joy, of the sweated, harsh deliverance, and all that would otherwise deprave made intercession for the flowered invitation of her being; its sovereign might within her, directly stemmed of her bravery, and she quite alone, and humbly regal, amongst her sweltering instincts.

'Hey you know you zonked out on me last night,' she said,

in her American accent tinged then with uncertainty. And in all that formed her voice there was now a tone of new, beloved possession. It was warm and protective. 'You really did too,' she added to his endearing look. And somewhere, somewhere in her voice, some few years ago and still sounding, he heard again a child's feet stamp in bold exasperation at an uncomprehending world; and all the silence of the wearied, the almost forced, forebearance, that humbly followed.

In love with her, his eyes smiling into hers, he believed he saw there the lagoon of her soul, that there he saw the silently changing colours reflect her solemn awareness of his need for her, of her active patience to the growth and direction of his need. Yet her eyes also held a prime and defiant assurance, and he needed to breach that, needed to enrapture her soul, and hear it utter its presence.

'Why did you come back to England?' he asked.

She laughed. Then for a moment turned her smiling face towards the gathering darkness of the street. Then she answered, innocently unanxious of his need for her, of her sensed knowledge of that need, of the headless savagery of his lust for her, that his savageness, clothed, was utmost between them, and raw, and stalking in her a presence mysteriously other than herself. He needed live possession of her slewing, delighted body. He needed the slim, young nudity of her body to vie against him for the joy beyond brute joy that languished in her; languished there in her, its joy patiently straining to be touched and reared and held, and struggled into her sensed body, and as reared and directly struggled into his body. There, joy became incarnate, potent, and wordless. To each a pristine beauty of its own deliverance, and each held its ecstasy in an immaculate joy.

The young woman spoke of her upbringing in the United States. She was the fifteen-year-old daughter of a drunken, American soldier and a drunken, G.I. English bride. That's how it seemed to her. And when her parents parted, her mother, for spite alone, had taken her back to England. And within her mother's ambit of domination, the new location had brought no change. The girl told her story of childhood woe as if it were an experience unique to her alone, yet still a childish, a lesser thing, than this new adulthood, as if her childhood hatreds and loves were miniatures, not mature and full-bodied of themselves, but little things, no more than seeds, and now, in adulthood, of no further importance.

Her lover nodded his anxious agreement. She reposed in him so much trust, and all of its unquestioning strength of attentive adoration of animal trust like a child's. Exactly like a child's. Yet against his will he thought only of her body, and thought of it in terms of burglary. Words and thoughts and images cascaded into life in his mind, new vistas of his own desires appeared, and each word-seeking thought dallied in its rush to unveil, partly, yet more and further, voluptuous needs. And in the wake of each there was a hushed tremble of guilt and fear. Fear that his need was beyond even the most indulgent understanding, fear that it was lascivious, perverse, and foul.

Yet he had had her; he had had her delicate, ungentle, acutely loving sexuality enclasped to his clasping body, had heaved and fallen with her when her sexual happiness, like a suddenly wounded bird in flight, strove to climb higher, climbed higher, then shook itself and fell tumultuously to a long, struggled, instant death.

It had been less than eighteen hours ago, the time where the girl was now in her story. Alone, wandering in the corridors of a huge, neglected shelter for the homeless of London. Behind her, the squat complacency of her mother. And in the girl, great, undirectable energies fretting for sovereignty. Somewhere she had read of these long, dark nights of transiency, of the fall from grace, and the expulsion from the child's lusty, innocent self into its displaced sense of bewildered loss, its sudden lack of direction, purpose, and knowledge on the new terrain of its newly born adulthood. She just didn't know which way to turn, everything seemed stupid and frivolous and irritating. And she banged doors and made noise just to distract herself. Then she had seen him, the elusive night-watchman, less than a handful of years older than herself. He looked lost, and her energies and attention focussed onto him, and intimately needed him, needed him with a harsh longing for her own joy.

Someone had heard their love-making. Her gloating mother had rushed to again humiliate her. And her now ensconced young man had later smacked the fat old cow with his closed fist. Thankfully, the young woman now snuggled closer to him, and squeezed his hand.

The young man was quietly and numbly distraught. He did not want this solemn trust. He did not want to hear her praise an act that shamed him. And now he heard that her brother and sister had also fled from home, years ago, and in the same manner that she had fled tonight. And she was joyous for the existence she imagined now awaited her. Yet to this rendezvous she had brought no baggage, except this awesome baggage of dependant trust. And he felt, irking wordlessly in his mind, the fear that he had become his own desires', and his own love's, first victim, and that it must be inevitably so. He could not hold so much of another's trust. All of the day had been spent in a matrix of thought that dwelt directly on the girl, on the love and the sexual delight she had given him, and, in giving, tacitly promised to give again; her love and her sexual delight, her independent, sexual delight. He could not be her saviour. She must know that. Yet he was so sexually aroused for her, had been so for so long, and he had assumed it was priceless.

Then he was aware that the girl had finished her story, and was alertly attentive to his silence.

When he spoke his voice escaped his control, but he was already nervously asking, against the prime intent of his thoughts, in stammering, broken politeness, if she would like a meal and some wine before going to the hotel. And his arched nervousness, the strangled pitch of his voice, grated out the invitation in a manner of thin, bored affectation. And the young woman's eyes, those luminous, swan-white eyes, anxious and curious, opened so vulnerably wide, and searched his face.

'Don't worry about Mum,' she said. 'She spent half her life belting me a lot harder than you hit her.' Then her eyes focussed, too quickly. 'You're not sorry are you? I mean about me, about meeting me?'

'Oh no, no. Not at all.'

She believed him, and smiled, and again her hand warmly squeezed his.

His body was heaving through the normal motions of walking, heaving through the pretence of smiling and talking. The

evening street noises were too high, too pitched, there was no
coherence to the movements, the reasons, the actions, of any
of the people out that night. Everything they did was make-
believe, was dressage, was pesade. Only by the most intense,
private acting could he forget the fear of an imminent, unchal-
lengeable humiliation. As if his presence on the street with
this girl, this woman, needed to be accounted for, and made
legal.

'Hey, what are you thinking of?' she asked, with all of her
native, preparatory intelligence.

Then, with plain nervousness that beguiled her and made
her smile, he told her of his plans; they would spend this
betrothed, solitary night of their lives in a first-class hotel,
and tomorrow, in holiday leisure, seek a place to establish and
begin their life together.

She didn't reply. Her face was replete with solemn, fresh,
unroughened maturity. Her arm linked and tightened around
his, and the side of her body rubbed its innocence and heat
sedately against him.

Their night passed. And in its expense of spirit, in its most
wrung satiety of sexuality, there was no aftermath of guilt,
nor of woe. She proposed a joy, and gave it bliss of proof with
love, delight, and passion. Many of his anxieties and guilts
vanished within him. And with her sleeping body next to
him, her pledged, trusting, sleeping body snuggled to him, he,
then, and for the first time, loved her, and loved her also as if
she were, indeed, a child.

Later, in moments of lulled wakefulness, he learned of the
open dreams, dexterity, and variety of her sexual longings.
And of her readied and anxious acceptance of their fulfilment.
In relieved return he whispered to her many of his most
darkened, secret desires. And in response she giggled, giggled
tightly and intensely to herself, then held his face and smilingly
looked upon him as a baby, the most deprived of babies.

Their night passed, in all the normal spectacularities of
new lovers.

Before noon the next day they left the hotel, and the reality

of their short life together, its commonplace familiarity of
happiness, dreariness, boredom, and domestically controlled
exasperations and lusts, routinely began.

And with diligence and much expense they found, before
the end of that afternoon, a bedsitter to rent. Its existence
immediately snared so many of their possibilities. Its size, its
expense, its concept as a habitat instantly showed the front line
of the already besieged, crowded barricades of a murderous,
grinding, endless war. A war fought by other means and by
proxy, a war that all fought, that most were doomed to lose,
that all were fighting as a means to live; a war whose soldiers'
power was financially brokered among the classed ranks of
human beings, where class was wealth and power, still feudally
used but rarely used with feudally unashamed display. It was
a war where anguish and tragedy were secreted. And it appeared
to be a bloodless war once the anguish, and the letting of
life's blood, was one or more removes from the spoils.

In the landlord's courteousness there was a salesman's tinge
of a whored, professional joviality. The landlord and the
couple smilingly exchanged names to each other; and the act,
so reminiscent of truth, gave total verisimilitude to the pretence each acted for the other. Pleasantries were exchanged,
wishes were exchanged, and all were of the same simulated,
ephemeral importance. As if neither landlord nor couple could
locate each other's individual reality, and so they generalised
each other, to the oblivion of each other, and of meaning. As
if an affair of grossness was being surreptitiously handled. As
if two entrenched and muddied foot-soldiers of opposing
classes suddenly saw, in their most intense moment of combat,
each other's humanity. Then the deposit and the rent money
were handed over, and all was complete.

The door was closed. There was silence, an alchemic silence.
The young girl said the Irish and English were a strange lot.
Then she settled to examining the room, and talkatively
began to create and to conjure out its many possibilities. She
was sombre and pragmatic, and thankful for this rented space
of privacy. It was enough for her. The young man enviously
watched and listened, and wondered how he had come to this
unplanned for, this now unwished for and unwanted, settled,
and already stagnant, condition in his life. The young woman's

cheerfulness grew more free, and still more free. She was growing delighted. And the young man, out of respect for her happiness, put aside his own misgivings.

Hours passed, and hours later the couple, under the unshaded glow of the light bulb, were happily squatted on the bed and eating their commingled portions of fish-and-chips. And in their scattered talking and laughing they were replete, all their private, and their individual, trepidations and worries banished to another day.

Morning came with its sudden beauty of slumber slowly, deliciously, dissolving. The young man felt his cleared mind stir about in happy drowsiness, and blinked open his eyes to the blinking, opening eyes of the young woman as she lithely moaned and stretched comfortably in the enjoyment of the bed. They smiled, and drowsily greeted each other to the new day.

Cats are called cats, and it suffices, until they become possessions. Then they are further nominated pet names, and these names respond to their owner's make-believe of reality, his fictive truth, the fictive truth he creates as he endlessly tries to form his world to the templet of his own, pragmatic fantasies.

And of all the fantasies of herself and her possibilities that the young woman had dallied with and enjoyed in her mind, her given name, and her received name, had never, in their own singular right, been possibilities of speculation. She saw all of all she was through the templet of her name, answered and addressed herself entirely through it. It was the most deep and fast, intimate milieu of her identity.

But to the young man, from the commencement of his adolescence, changes of name were almost seasonal, and no name was allowed to hold or encompass his own identity of himself. Names were anchors to times and places past, and often, deliberately, he cut them adrift, and left behind all of their glories and their guilts. Then they faded to the relevancy of old photographs, of daguerreotypes of the place and condition of the times of his life. And it detached him from the empty uselessness of his past, opened his future to its new gaols and allowed him, sometimes, to opaquely see himself in the past as others, then, must have seen him, and must have seen most lucidly through him. He could smile at the titled, stilted lithographs, muse about the stranger there, observe the quaintly hidden motives and the intent of his displayed, passed, distanced, self. And sometimes he then learned something of what he had been; then sometimes gained an understanding of what he now was, the stranger recognising his own familiarity in another stranger, the stranger he most honestly still was to himself; to the entity that reflected upon its own self because it did not know its own self.

But the young woman, named as a strange, unknown language is familiarly named on the tongue, yet is still strange, unspeakable, held in her eyes a beloved, unspeakable mystery, the magnificent and inexplicable lagoon of her soul and her self, and all their vulnerable seasons. To map and chart this, to give it a name that magically reflected its colours and depths, was to use hopelessly the sway of fresh, beautiful words, and unsought rhetoric, to simulate a virginal image in the mind of the glories and the art, quite unutterable, of beauty in the mind's eye.

She could mingle her native, fluent intelligence with rapid lies, and without malice, and stumble over a quick, petty lie into immediate contradiction, and embarrassment. Then smile, and into the smile's bashfulness came the tenderness of all her private, reluctant truths.

But now she frightened at the thought of lying to a bureaucrat. That she could so easily change her name, age, and nationality amazed her. Such possibilities of self-naming seemed numbing. A few added years were little to the space of freedom they created, the new nationality as artificial as the original, but for the name, her new name, she had to search for the right fit. She could not happily settle on any name, any age, any nationality. And the attempt almost jerked the originals out of fit. That was an odd feeling for her, to feel unhoused in that way. But over breakfast in the dripping-lard camaraderie of a British working-class café, the young man coaxed her into changing her official pet name, and her age, and her nationality. Then he coached her into making her believe it, as if it had all become second nature, as easily and as unthinkingly as the originals. She really did not, but his straining patience imposed on her a solid acceptance of the new facts.

For solid moments. Solid, isolated moments that never congealed into firm, forming, and forgotten beliefs. She couldn't believe in her own fictive truth, this young woman, from that land of strange fruit where nations as equally glorious as the Saxons, the Teutons, the Latins, the Celts, and all the rest, had been magically turned by manifest destiny into tribes, and having lost their just battles were then savagely unfit to survive. Our perception, a fixed distortion, of attributes ignorant of essence, the fall of history's die faced down, and so no tired, huddled masses of Iroquois nor Apache nor others yearning to breath free. And their fate, their oblivion, became the strangest fruit of American civilization and American fiction. And so we have no dime-store Europeans renowned for drunkenness, and many sad tales of old, past glorious. If our past is a fixed distortion of reality so is out bloody present.

The young woman looked amazed at the snap of his impatience. She laughed, but it was tense laughter, and the young man heard it as a veil over her hurt feelings. It was most accomplished. It seemed to him as if the contours of her psyche, the very compression of her psyche, was a repertory of parts moulded from books and movies, most obviously from movies. The long, dark night of transiency, this fall from grace, from the peaceful child's lusty loves and hates to the adolescence's self-shame, this paraphrase he could not trace. But the rest, the poses, the postures, even the act of love and sex, the grimaces and the gasps, the graticule of clichés that most of her thoughts appeared to come from, these were all of Hollywood's indoctrinating, model portraits. And such a cultured young American woman couldn't grasp the importance of her own self-created fiction, as if its presence must threaten some vitally precious aspect that was unique and central to her, as if the fictive truth of her given pet name made her unique, and she cherished and clung to it for its veil of uniqueness, its veil of many childish things that now lived more strongly and seriously in the adult than they ever did in the child. The mystery was how much of her self she had come to invest, and to repose, in her name, but not, somehow, in herself, as if she were all of the imagined shorthand of her name, and she nothing else, then, than a named cipher.

The young woman looked lost and pensive, and stared at the cup that she nestled between the palms of her hands. Countless times he had seen that pose demonstrated by movie actresses. It was a fiction that made her not at all herself. It made of her a living cliché of someone else's imagination. It would have consequences. She'd never know, in the crushed space of sentient life between oblivion and oblivion, who uniquely and inimitably she most namelessly was; she'd never know her faculties, never nurse and rear them to her own likeness, and she'd forever keep the unrepeatable truth of her life, the corpse of her still-born self, buried within her, and rotting everything there within her very passable sham of life.

The aspect of her face changed, and he saw her human misery. It was a genuine, self-created expression; it held that touch of frightened sanity in it. The young woman said she just wouldn't know who she was, just wouldn't know, wouldn't know what to expect, of herself, of anything, anything at all.

And from a face that was still lovely, and whose dimensions hadn't changed, a wide aspect of broken vulnerability appeared, and dominated the face. It held a space where identity, true, self-discovered identity, ought to have occupied and held, occupied fully and unrootably held there. Without it the features of her face were purposeless; lacked an immediacy of co-ordinated verve, and lost their objective beauty into a limp blandness.

He apologised to her, and looked away, sadly. After a calculated moment he whispered that if she changed her age by a few months, perhaps, for safety, by an extra year, if she would change her name to stop her mother's spite pursuing them, then he would be less tense, less prey to the shadowy, snapping fears and anxieties that insecurity produced. He would feel protected.

She responded, smilingly, and agreed. And in her agreement made it clear that she could not, alone, go to the necessary offices. To this one demand she now clung with a great, limp, heavy force. He protested that it was unnecessary, and in reply the tone of her voice pitched, and he could hear again, still sounding, the echo of the child's feet stamping their lusty demands for power. Yet it now incited in him the desire, not to frolic and delight with her, and to make love to her, but to take her and spank her, to make her obedient to an illusive, maddening rationality, to bring her back, by shock, to her senses.

At least, and immediately, aiding him with one concession, she immediately changed its manner into a new demand from which he could be released only by foregoing the first concession. And this, for the moment, he had to accept. But it rankled, it scratched, it irked him. For the first time he was aware of the matched deceit of their relationship, the lie that passion and love were ends, and not means.

He smiled, and agreed. And with slim, nude obedience she reached and squeezed his hand, and thanked him. She was now happy, and her happiness flowed unhindered directly to him. If he conformed to her minimum criterion of expectation, all of her happiness, and all of the happiness she had to give, would be given freely in direct return. It was an instinctive settling of expectations, an instinctive drafting of a personal accord, to which love and desire were not key, but adjunct. Most centrally it was an understanding of what each could expect of the other's best and worst. It was in a language of all of the senses, combined at once of eyes, looks, sounds, and of physical responses fathoming beyond the reach of common understanding. And in its first squall of understanding, it became exclusive. Only these, the begetters, the emotional signatories, would understand its innate moral force and power over them and to them, its possibilities for forgiveness, for perception and release, and its minute, private terms to differentiate each degree and each limit of their responses to each other.

The young woman led the way out of the café, and the young man followed.

He accompanied her to an employment agency, and sat next to her during the brief application process. The young woman smiled too warmly, and too much, at the clerk. She whispered too anxiously, too obediently, as if she were, years ago and still sounding, knowingly repeating a caught lie, whispering, and desperately wishing it would become true, trying to wish it true, obediently displaying her self-disgust, and now she was still obediently continuing that punishment of self-debasement that had commenced years before when she was, innocently, a good little girl. She now moved about too much on her chair, was too flighty, and, in unconscious, darting motions, kept touching and holding the young man's hands and body. All the clients, and all the interviewers, were women. And in some of their watching eyes the young man saw a preparatory curiosity, and a conceit, as they looked at the young woman, seemed to value themselves against her, and found her less than they.

Yet her presence somehow recommended him, as if her trust made him a measured, and an acceptable, threat. He could feel their randiness for him, their vicarious randiness and passion for him, and instinctively smelt it stem from their aroused rivalry, their dismissive bitchiness, towards the young woman. Yet it was a very pleasurable feeling, and it pleased him.

The feeling was already satisfied and slipping into formed experience before he felt the savoury aftertaste suffuse his ego. It was alive and gloating itself in his mind; and its verbal simulation there was smug, rather smug, and, more rather still, rather cocky.

Innocent of all this, the young woman was given a blue introduction card. On it was her new name, and the name and address of a restaurant in north London. After they'd travelled there, and she'd gotten the job as a waitress, the employer put some more information from her directly onto the card. And easily and quickly the fictive truth on the card was becoming bureaucratic, ultimate truth. At the local government office they accepted the blue card, stamped it, and gave it back to her to mail to the agency. And they promised to send to her new employer all the necessary papers for her first job. She was so young, so innocent, so anxiously on the fringe of nervousness in her timid dealings with them, and so, so timidly eager, in her entrance into the adult world, as they once were, that they saw themselves in her, smiled warmly for the memories they saw in her innocence, smiled their encouragement, and wished her luck.

She smiled in return, but to her the world was empty of

meaning. She held the smile transfixed to her face, and left the office. There was now, in the listlessness of her discontent, a newly raw awareness of the fears and happiness frozen within her, and of the distant sea of human potential frozen within her. There was no sense of a freedom gained. It was a sudden, harsh discovery of her exile, and of its distance from her potential. It was the touch of a young, freshly dying autumn, and its unquiet, dead leaves reeking of the insignificance of all things. And most acutely, pitted to a knot of anxiety in her stomach, there was the freshly raw understanding of the insignificance of herself, and of her previously named place in the world. She had discovered the freedom of the rejected, of the excluded. She no longer knew, in any way, how much of herself belonged, uniquely and inalienably, to herself. Her self was a lonely and a hidden thing, frightened and childishly cowed within her. It was surrounded by lost loneliness, a vast, softly-pressured loneliness held still in an empty, unresisting space. It was a self she seemed now to sense behind her actions, but a self she had yet to see, a self she had yet to coax into open, growing, conscious life.

She had become a silent, distant place in the world. Looking out, it seemed to her a frantic and senseless place. All of the people in the street, and the young male beside her, were of great, massive, physical substantiality, a hard, demanding, struggling substantiality, but of no significance at all. And none showed, by any manner, any pressing consciousness. Looking out, the activities of people seemed of massive substantiality, but inert, frantically inert, to a purpose that was transubstantial to themselves, and to their activities.

She felt herself separate from the world, yet she felt herself whole, and autonomous, in a strangely raw, vulnerable way. Something strange brushed repulsively against the side of her face, and she instantly recoiled from it. And in that distracted instant she looked back sideways in disgust and saw, stunned in its motion, the retreat of the playfully inquiring hand of the young man, and saw the risen surprise in his eyes. Where once there had been a cosmopolitan brightness in his eyes there was now a still bright but uncosmopolitan look, the empty and lost-freedom look of a vagrant. And in her eyes it exposed him. She knew the thought created bizarre expressions, but he was not, named or nameless, what she had thought he was. He was not who or what he thought or imagined himself to be. It was as if his entirety was forever based on the wrong assumptions about himself. But there was always that peculiar aspect in the Irish, in the Irish who seemed to forever throng the globe in search of work. She had been traipsed around enough American and British cities and towns to have noticed its commonality, the American Mick who was flattered to be more apple-pie than any Chuck, and the British Paddy who was flattered to be more cor blimey than any Cockney, and the Emerald Isle Irish with their endless and neurotic nationalism and patriotism. If you were Irish, and not one of these, you had no frontier to hide behind, and you were lost. And he was lost, and he was weaker than her, and he clung to this as if it were freedom. There was now insight in her love of him, and it altered her love. She felt, and knew that she felt, a slight departure between her best interests and her bosom interests.

'I thought this day would never come,' she said, and reached out a hand to touch his face. She told him of the fear, and the sense of self-betrayal she had felt in the entire charade, how memory locked itself against recall, except for unexpected, squeamish recollections of panic and discomfiture in the employment agency, how the sound of the first whispered lie roared itself deadeningly back against her face. And all was now shrouded in a vague, hazy silence. Now there was a deep hiatus between her and her previous life, between her and some other aspect of her mind. She felt more recognisable to herself, as if a long amnesia had passed, and she had rendez-voused with her self again, and felt again the entire stretch of her possibilities and her limitations. There was an awakened pragmatism and clarity, a feeling of unshadowed sanity. It could not be false. There was no hint of self-perjury in it, no hint of believing her inner lies to herself.

And these green, little thoughts, for their existence and for their content, were as cheerful to her as the sight of sprigs and single blades of grass pushing to life through the universal concrete of received values, of received identities, of received names. And this young, and not fully tried freedom, could be easily crushed. Yet she enjoyed the sense of delicacy in her

words, the hesitation and the stress, the process of delibera-
tion and construction, and the tender beginnings there of a
settled understanding of herself. It was as if she had heard the
unenterable silence of her existence, but there was nothing
frighening or eerie in its substance. She had to frail with
insufficient words, with bits and pieces of words, and gesture,
and chase nuance and understanding with the quick of her
eye, and speak sparingly, speak voluminously, with precision
and with delicate lack of precision, and all just to let him
know the echo of her growing, distant self that she so magically
heard.

And lovingly, with her young, tender awe of love, it never
occurred to her that she was bearing a tale of paradise that
he had never heard before. And somehow, as she spoke, his
mind had to reach ahead of her, and greet her in agreement at
each intermittent step of her arrival. He looked at her admir-
ingly, with envy, and wondered how much of himself he must
forever keep hidden from her. He had to keep her convinced
that he was where he now pretended to be, and he had also
to catch up with her and really be there. It required too much
of him, and too quickly. He felt the fear of losing, felt the
sudden, internal fall into a void of defeat growing in his
stomach, and his nervousness rekindled itself into resurgent,
dominant control. He had always circumvented his fears, never
advised nor forced himself to seek them out, to tremble and
humiliate himself, the sacrifice needed for acknowledgement
and understanding in the victorious combat against them. And
in circumventing his fears he had succeeded, and succeeded
in narrowing his life into a tiny, private, never before spoken
of, kernel of despair.

The young woman pensively listed some household items,
and the groceries, that she needed to buy. She then said that
he had to find work, and he nodded. She stopped, looked in
a strained manner about the street, and looked directly at
him. She smiled, and the smile showed the power with which
she was overcoming another fear.

'I'm goddamn broke,' she said. And in relief he passed
across the wad of his savings. She took some, and passed it
back.

'Thanks,' she said, and kept on smiling. And so plainly, in

the natural flow of her smile, she showed that she had not transferred her anxieties or her fears, but at great and frightening cost confronted them, and so unexpectedly to herself, but so powerfully, won. It bestowed on her an ease and an authority. It showed, and would always show, its dignity, and its humility.

She moved a hand upwards to correct some flaw in the lie of his shirt collar. And her hand was moving again, for some further retouching of his appearance, when she stopped in mid-motion, hesitated, and in that hesitation he became conscious of his recoiling fear pulling him back from her concerned hand. For a moment, before he could gather any understanding, his face shocked empty of expression, stared at her. And with a strained deliberatedness he then joked at her with his face. Her unhesitatingly happy manner returned, and returned with no scar of its moment's absence. Yet the farewell canted, went uncontrollably from pitch to pitch without any gain of resonance to its purpose, as if it might, and forever, part them as newly made strangers to each other. He abruptly turned away, turned ungainly and out of step to his will, and heard, shrilling behind him, her humoured, companionable, buoyant giggle.

All of the joyous turmoil, all of the unslaked, new possibilities of adventure, all were now hers. As if, in becoming her lover, he had become aged, and was now custodian to her youthful growth. For the first time ever he felt the awesome speed with which the young catch up on their elders. And it chilled him. His life lay as silently as a new grave, and he felt its eerie, dead presence.

But the city of London was prosperous, and there was work to be had. There was that solid, visible, achievable objective, and he lazily turned his mind to it. It was a mere process of applying at any of the factory gates. When he did so his mind was concentrated elsewhere, and so, without nervousness of the process he applied, without his obsessive self-consciousness focussing him neurotically alert to the absence of human meaning, to the process of an employer's hireling sizing him up a dumb asset, the necessary lack of humane discourse in the process, its banter and its jargon, the direct thrust of its necessary questions, and he complied, obediently, quietly, and thoughtlessly, the goods for necessary sale now on necessary display, at the precise level of a foreman hiring muscle at a factory gate, a process that would, by any utterance of acknowledgement, leave both enraged in the spoken subjugation of their humanity, and the distance from that to common joy and delight.

He was back on the street, his mind just starting to clear, and it was already all over. He had a job, and therefore sustenance, and the ability to buy, week by week, his weekly necessities, as the days spent him, emptied him of life, and day by day his future. These casual jobs, plentiful, and monotonously easy to get, offered only the most shadowy purchase on the present, and none at all on the future. He turned away the thought. It was of no moment, certainly not of this moment. And it might never be of moment. There might be distractions, massive, hypnotic distractions from the self-consciousness of knowing, moment by unfilled moment, that his life, almost always empty of contentment, of achievement and of its ease, was forever slipping past, and falling deeper into the growing and readied grave of all past days. O never, never, to be an ageing spectator of his own past, never to have that as his current, futureless present. Moments are hard, solid, substantial things, eternal in time, and forever indifferent to our use of them, and all we believe we achieve and attach to them is to them wholly fictional. Yet he could not house these moments, didn't know how to concentrate them, how to concentrate himself to a life-line of moments, how to force and shape them to a purpose vital and of salvation for himself. A life of its own impetuous purpose and delight, even a jungle savage's wanton, brute acceptance of life and its necessary circumstances, even these distractions, as massively useful as any fantasticism, an urban savage's brute strength or guile of conviction, and their common contentment of ignorance, even these nimbly escaped his grasp, and his desire.

It, the lack of a solid, wrenching purchase on the structure and direction of his life, was of the most eminent moment. But other than the normal, working-class response of sharp banditry, of hustling of some sort, no answer showed itself within the confined grope of his question. All he had was an endlessly sweaty, dirty grasp on muscular, slavish jobs. There

was not there, and could never be, even a shadow of fulfilment
and purpose. And he had this young American girl whom he
loved for her frolicsome sexuality, her raised, taut body
unrippling, her stretched and suddenly stammering little feet
of scampering sexuality, and all of her motley, stippled, piebald
pleasures as she schooled him to the arts of her pleasure. But
that, even that, shared in a rented room during hours culled
from lives of otherwise meniality, even that pleasure, denied
its proper environs for nourishment and maturity, could, must,
turn sour, turn to taunt and to madden.

It was hard to think of that room as home, the place where
they would nourish their values, the place where they would
find recuperation and development. Home was where they
would be formed and directed to the entire thrust of their
potential, not a place where they would be kenneled and
trained by brute circumstance. But at the precise level of a
park bench, or the level above of a bedsitter, home is another
word for despair, and the incarnation and the host of all of
despair's attributes.

Yet often, and often with the utmost contentment, he had
slept on park benches, lived in hovels. And they were not
offensive to his sense of dignity. It often had the most subtle
macho pride, and the romance, the romance of the tragic loser,
and the deflective glamour of its real sadness. Life had not
then been a wasted, headlong fall through the vast and empty,
unusable-to-effect, expanses of time. Some long-forgotten
mistake, or omission, and he was forever mis-directed, quite
aimless, in life. And left to spend all his adolescence, and all
of the youngness of adulthood, aimlessly seeking that mistake,
that omission within. Yet previously it had created no void
within him, no sense of the void of departure coldly alive in
his stomach. Measured against the young woman's solid and
increasingly quick advancement, his life was wanting. As if he
lived, wounded and huddled within life, but lacked the courage
to raise himself, to even move at all.

The young woman could not fail to find better than he
had to offer. She had every chance of finding the best. And if
he stayed alone, stayed to himself, there was always the pensive enjoyment, however sad, of privately licking past and
present wounds. It was a hypocritical dignity, but vestural

where there was nothing else. And he could endure it, even suck occasional pleasure from it. Alone, he could spare himself the unmeetable sight of his reflection in her slowly opening eyes as she more and more saw through the staunch lies of his facade to the hollowness in which he lived, to the waste land of his inadequacies, and the tutoring of his hopes, all the unacknowledged midnight wishes and determination to surpass his present limits and gain the potential he felt, in the midnights, were within him, and waiting only for the proper régime, of attitude, or thought, or behaviour, or somesuch, to be fully released as his inalienable attributes, all these petty, uncollected wishes were again his, again constituted his best hope, and were best safeguarded, for development, in a solitary life. When all these long-postponed and long-untended private visions of his real and true self had been nurtured and tutored until the only labour remaining was the labour of harvest. Then he could be free, honest, and at peace, and willing to fully expose to another, and to give, the intimacy of his private self. Till then it was too raw. It had to remain in the young, huddled sanctuary within. And only there, unspoken, was its safety assured. In time, in the gentlest privacy, it might unfold itself into an indestructable presence. But before that, anyone close, anyone at all close, might sense it and discover it, in all of its limp-lipped, mealy-mouthed abjectness. And even a lover might, in repulsed reaction, or bytimes, accidentally, even playfully, or in the quick heat of spite, might sneer at it, might scorn and laugh it huddling back irretrievably to the realm of exposed, inner defeat. There it would move no more, and always, always, keep its eyes tightly closed.

Yet what he sought to protect he could not name: an idealised, imagined vision of himself, a self that could play and sport in his personality, be formative to almost all of his personality, but instantly vanish when reality returned from the daydreamed midnights of sport and play. It happened too quickly and was already done, moment by rapid moment, in a hail of moments that shaped out the reach and the substance of his life. Looking back, he watched himself, and saw what they had made of him. And all those moments, always, gone before he could grasp any. Only in the heated moment of anger or lust was there a grasped congruency, a full intercourse, with the moment, with animate existence, and its sense of vast and great purpose, reality, and depth; and of his active place therein. Life otherwise was an ascent of last moments, each showing the pilgrimage of what he once had been, where he had once been. But there was no sense of texture, of feel, of smell in those past visions of himself. He could as simply have imagined them. And at the end of each looking back there was, moment by moment, fixed hard in his mind and stomach, an anguished caw of exile, of departure, not from the self he saw there, but from all those forever-past moments. Then he found himself alone, with the present, and its exiled vacancy of himself. And in that wilderness he could relate more to his imagination than to his past.

He had to imagine. To know himself, as he was, different to his life, he had to imagine. Had to imagine a self, had to find or create himself in his imagination, was otherwise insensate to the first-hand feel of existence; had to imagine in order to know the beginnings of himself, to know his awareness of himself. Even his learned knowledge had to be again processed in imagination, made interanimate with imagination, before it became intimate and vibrant to his being. Yet imagination gave a common, continuous substance to him and made his reality assessable. It was barely explainable to himself, could not be sanely shared with another. He must never trust the entry of another into this confidence. And he could not think this without believing the same of the young woman. Yet each time he looked into her eyes, into the lagoon of her soul, his feelings and love were moved by a guide that was inalienably sexual, or was otherwise as gawking as an idiot's bewilderment at her strange, featous beauty, and the lingering, flickering, deep mystery there in her soul's lagoon. He must never, ever, dabble with the soul he imagined there. It was there that imagination slammed shut the door on the sport and play of reality, and permitted reversed entry, and at the greatest peril, only to itself, to its own querying in itself of itself. To do otherwise, to enter, querying or not, into another's imagination, to madden it by his disturbing, altering presence, was also to go out of his mind, to go where he could never again find or retrieve any idea, any image, any identity of himself.

The stretch of thought brought him nowhere. It gave him

no purchase on his condition and predicament. He longed, on the edge of despair, to totally enter into the young woman, to strip himself there of memories, of his failed knowledge of life, of his weariness, of his lost and wasted years, and then to sleep within her closed protection, to awaken there his self-esteem.

If only they could have occupied for a while a space of unpressed time, a place unsweated and unhurried by the demands of work and the wherewithals of existence, where reality was excluded and where they were free, bountiful with each other, playful and talkative, a place to frolic with their imaginations and their possibilities, a place of unpressed space and time to use with the endless strength and power of their sexuality to create a period of occupied grace in which other tentacles of attachment could grow and fasten between them. Then the divisive myth between them of a given reality that was external and indifferent to them, a reality then differently perceived and differently experienced by each, would disappear as an impediment, and a common, bonded reality of themselves emerge with their changing, reforming selves. Yet even the thought, the clarifying of the impediment, then made of its resolution a scheming subterfuge, formalised, artificial, and false. It ought to have happened before either was aware of it. It could not happen now without contrivance, and with contrivance it was empty and useless and worthless. And so its nourishing truth was never to be enjoyed and experienced by him.

Yet he still wanted rid of the young woman. Within him, he still deeply pined to find someone, pined for the expression of a physically shared love and acceptance, and gave his longing's unholdable surfeit, gladly, to the first who accepted it. But it was a longing so intense, and so smothered by a man-like, sthenic shame, that he had to give it to someone, anyone. And he always gave it dismissingly, and uselessly, surreptitious even to his own pragmatic volition. The giving brought about a relief that was not only sexual, yet in the young woman's responses there was not, however hard he tried to deceive himself, there was not a matched reciprocity of understood, consummated unity. Its lack made him acknowledge his exposed, wounded loneliness in his own existence.

He felt very distant from hope. The future offered him an ordeal of inanimate, mundane years ahead, an already-past, dead time. And the self-induling passions of appetite and habit, the unsimple, stylized pleasures of the poor, would pass him along through the drudgery of unwanted years. A shudder came into his senses, and he felt the retuse presence of all of his guilts, uncertainties, and doubts, felt himself slumped and gutted of hope. Betrayed and defeated before he had learned of the battle in life, the battle for worked, rewarding harvested life, before he had even learned in his gut of life's moment by moment finality, his alive and squirming defeat in conscious existence was sealed. He felt fear, fearful for himself in all the hard, barren years ahead. And hopelessness staked itself in the pit of his stomach. He stood and consciously felt the anxiety, a numbed panic of anxiety, bleed itself inside him.

In that observed consciousness he found a vague leverage against the fear that silently clanged against all of his reason and instinct. And he needed alcohol, needed whatever nourishment, strength, and consolation, whatever numbing sedation of fear it could bring.

But there was no alcohol for sale at that hour in the afternoon. It was a minor and otherwise unimportant detail of life in London, yet now all his doubts, hesitancy, and anxieties immediately transferred themselves to it, and made its resolution a test of his personal worth. His validity now focussed itself into beating the odds and getting a bottle of whisky.

Without preparatory thought he entered a store. It was a self-service store, but the tobacco and alcohol were held behind the check-out desk. He asked the man there for a bottle of whisky, and noticed at once a stereotyped aversion and contempt for alcohol and its users come into the man's eyes. The man was an Asian, and an attitude of new power proudly showed in him. It was imitative, directly imitative of a gloating in the cruelty of the applied law, of the sahib's clean smugness in applying another's power, and incidentally his own warm lust, directly onto the native's back. The unconscious parody of a colonialist's insolence was such a numbing tragedy, so great a waste, and with no checked knowledge that insolence is the attitude of the master's deputy,

and the rebel's, of a caste of mind that understands no equality
of humanness, such re-embodied ghosts of colonialism so
plain in so obvious a victim held the young man amazed. And
in that fractional gap of attuition he knew that he had whispered his request, knew that he must ask again, and that he
could only whisper or shout. He knew the tension of other
sources, his entire life pouring its validity into this tension of
human contact, was about to snap. He had either to become
a creature of pure animal rage, or a shambles of a human being.
And he could not yet face that reckoning.

'I'm a drunken Irish pig you fucking idiot,' he screamed at
the man. 'Now give me the fucking bottle.'

The brown man looked at him, looked at him as if he saw
the wreck of a human being, was long habituated to the sight,
and knew, and shared, something of its source. The progeny
of defeated, conquered people, meeting as adversaries in their
ex-master's capital city, in a petty grocery store in that city,
and each knew too much about the other's shame, could
smell the lingering essence of that shame in the most remote
of cousins. Even the new native citizens of the United States,
even their buoyant self-confidence wavers near to an unhealed
inferiority when they confront Britishness on British soil.
And it is Britishness, not Englishness, it is that impossible-
to-question sense of identity, of prime identity and of primacy,
a nationalism so primitively pure that its sterling originality
can be no more than slavishly copied. But the taint of defeat,
of defeat never answered to its source by reciprocal occupa-
tion, is a most palpable, a still raw and a still throbbing reality.
That only the most thoughtful and concerned of the ex-
master's progeny understand this is the most enraging and
the lasting injustice of it all.

The bottle was wrapped in a brown paper bag and passed
across the counter. Then the vertical immensity of the wait
for change, after he clutched the bag, and a longing that the
storekeeper knew of the last vestiges of response that must
clutch, in drowning determination and delusion at this bag of
straws.

Back on the street, knowing that the alcohol would lull his
nerves while it dragged him further from his own help, the
young man unpicked the sealing foil from the bottle's cap,

undid the cap, and drank from the bottle, like, exactly like, a man trying to take nourishment at his own mirage. He had to leave the young woman. He had to return and tell her. Life, in its youth, in the full strength of its youth, is meaningless without a social identity that is at least congruent to the imagined, reflected self, and is useless without a firm purchase, a social, intellectual, and financial purchase on its quality and direction. Leisure is the munching enjoyment of the fruits of life, the surplus rewards of work, or of luck. Mere free time, without the wherewithal to obtain the fruits, to plainly see and know but never to attain, is unoccupied, tortured time, time whose slow cascade of seconds is a boundless, unwalled, close confinement of poverty. From his work he had no more than the grounded consolation of a common subsistence, and the shabby and kenneled accommodation of bedsitters. By scrimping even on this income he sometimes hoarded small sums of money, and then, randomly, and with a rapidity that always bewildered him, the tiny sums trickled through his fingers. A few rest days, a treat, and all was gone.

He was sitting by the side of the kerb. The alcohol had already gathered some sedation around the fear and cowardice in his mind, and a confidence, a shored confidence and indifference had started to form in him against any thought of the outward display he presented to the eyes of others. He cared about the opinions people might have of him, cared because he tended to betray himself and to form his responses favourably to those opinions, and to quite suddenly find himself even further away from his own solitary, self-figured self. There, in that misprison of himself, he was not himself, was not the truth of himself, and was forever uneased by his own self-perjury.

It was this the young woman might discover; not his lies to her, but his lies to himself. He had to be rid of her, to jettison her given body and soul, and her loving obedience; he had to dis-spirit all that he had strove so hard to possess. He knew he must hurt her to the soul of her being, yet not wound her. She would have to be prepared, have to be made a little wishful to be first rid of him. Then he could depart, unburdened, and in protective loneliness and solitude, and with great quietness and sanity, shred his fictions of himself, discard opinions and attitudes and habits, see lucidly and lucently to the truth of himself, and with wit, speed and accuracy of intellect, rear that truth for his image and likeness.

He was aware of no drunkenness in his thoughts. Thoughts came with the original, pristine impact of new, physical experience, and were as pleasing as fulfilled sexuality. His thoughts were more manageable. He needed words that formed to their manner of impress; cobblestone words, words that did not merely simulate the substance and presence of thought. Words draw a treacherous map of thought, pretend, by definition, to have thought's meaning, as if all combinations of words did indeed swiftly sum up all possible meaning, and could explain their, and our, mysteries. He felt as if he were a word, a spent word, and he laughed aloud. He tried to force a way through the chyme of his unworded self, to relieve the pressures that shaped and formed it, and then, by some magic, to make himself, to re-create his self in his own image and likeness. And there, just there, words did openly hold the live body of the thought. There, just there, words did not bury the thought, did not stake their presence as the commonplace grave-markers of thought; grave-markers, however poetic, solemn, or banal, and all words were also so, as if each word of thought was, once coined into acceptable currency, its own cliché; an undeveloped negative of the thought, and negative to the thought. And this conclusion filled and satisfied his mind.

The young man raised himself and strolled along the street. He held the open bottle by its neck in the brown paper bag. The street was a functional, dormitory, city street. Nowhere at all a flower, no sway of nature in its countenance. No hush, no bustle, of human magic. Yet he felt the distant presence of a lantern, its dim, new light secured. It might be the fool's confidence of drunkenness, but he was willing to accept its courage, to dance bizarre oddities in his mind, and to lighten his step. He could blink, relax his forehead, and trip lightly down the stairs to the underground.

He emerged into the daylight at Charing Cross Road, London's promiscuous university of bookshops forever intertwined with the area of brothels and sex-shops. The street arose, almost straight, almost uninterrupted, from the coil of abused side-streets, arose as if its shops were beacons that

gave to the otherwise lost an aura of settlement, of a purposeful, occupied place.

A magical passing of time commenced. The ductility of his
infant identity interwove itself with the ductility of a titled
book here, a book there, from bookshop to bookshop. His
slave's blood, the locked and chained spirit of his humanness
smelled itself. Elsewhere, in the swamp heat of sex, or in the
pulsating noise of the discothèque darkened and then distorted
by twists of neon lighting, the massed, youthful cravings for
an unseeing milieu of sexual exchange. There, in that placebo
of life, his slave's body could have found its dummy release in
the slow moving, then swaying, the then quickening symphony
of movements, the struggled release of the body's sexuality,
the groovy, shimmying release from humanness, from its
consciousness of its aching desires. And its jettisoned climax
of emptiness, of unfulfilment, of leftover disappointment, and
of a growing, imprisoning guilt.

But his unshackled awe in the possession of the books was
silent, and heated of nourishment and fulfilment. Here was
a slave whose saved pennies had purchased a temporary freedom, and whose mind sensed a way of permanent escape. He
ignored all thoughts of the day, the exact tomorrow, when his
drudged servitude must recommence. He dipped and browsed
in each book, and recoiled from the writerets who treated
their work as a branch of show business, a major or a minor
branch of show business, whose very words called literature a
hairshirt, knew no more, and continued their danced entry
on the minor slopes of show business. The summit of show
biz, and not literature, was their goal, and they wisely knew
it. Yet there were still many books of the invisible glory of
literature, and in each that he bought there were browsing
lines that resonated to his unnamed and unworded quest, lines
that seized at his imprisonment, held him railed against the
cold steel bars of ignorance that confined the grope of his
mind, made him aware of his groping humanness inside his
animal cage. And too soon the odd bags of books weighed
him down, and stopped him reaching for more.

Outside, the afternoon streets were already palled by
winter's early darkness, and time regained its pressure in his
mind. So, so many hours had passed. He walked slowly along,

his stride as gangly as a slave's under the displaced burdens of the bags of books. And his mind, too, not inter-assured of itself, had its inelegant gait. And it seemed, in one swerve of focus, to have become sober, and again paniced of its duties.

On that long, looped street of bookshops, and of sex-shops, there were some odd, rugged shops that sold surplus military clothing. And in one such shop he bought a military rucksack, then settled into the back of a sandwich restaurant and redistributed the books carefully among the maze of compartments in the holdall. And in all this arranging and re-arranging no one noticed how quickly he drank the soggy, milked tea from the plastic cup, how handily the empty beaker then stood discarded on the floor in the midst of emptying plastic bags, and the numbed gladness of his emotions when the whisky bottle silently filled the cup to the brim. No one saw how quickly and distastefully he drank the whisky, again refilled the beaker, slipped the whisky bottle into a side compartment, then straightened himself up, relieved, a chore well done, the better to enjoy the flood of sedation from the cup that was now occasionally and socially sipped.

People, human beings each of uniqueness within their common designation, people, sat in isolation or in isolated groups about the restaurant. Others came and went. And despite the artificial courtesies of greetings, of request and of service, the routined intercourse of strangers supplying each other with the wherewithals of their reciprocating demands, they were something other than blank strangers to each other. They were social fictions to each other, suppositions of each other that reflected neither observation or knowledge but each one's assumed, and instant, expectation of the other. People were of an unwalled zoo of humanness, of frightening, mascaron faces, and were literally made-up, by someone, by parents, by each other, by themselves. They were a make-believe of each other, a pastiche of each other's needs, ambitions, values. Everything about them was contrived, simulated, mimicked. Even their forms and expressions of intelligence were as rote learned as their language, and as deceptive of understanding. They generated mimicry, contrivance, and simulation, and had a definite knowledge of their own impression of themselves. Each, and including the young

man, had a dangerous sense of insight into others, could sur-
mise and appraise, as the young man was now doing, and
do so with an instinctive, deep, and anxious sense of their
correctness, of secular infallibility. They rushed to ceaseless
judgements of each other, and quickly knew the correct regime
of reformation. Yet none had such a governing, manipulative
understanding and insight of themselves. And all the young
man saw in others his observations demanded that he must
also see in himself.

With a sense of fixed maturity, a sense of its firm purpose,
he set out to discard all of his past, and its one living, still
breathing, mistake.

A smile of forgiveness tried to gather itself in the hurt, aching
face of the young woman. Delicate neatness distracted from
the room's over-used shabbiness. The newly bought cooking
utensils were stacked with consideration, and on the unfolded
card table a cold buffet was set. Around the girl, as if she were
its dark, mothering bud, all of the freshness and neatness of
the room had the aspect of a shy flower's leaf. So thoroughly,
quickly, and nimbly she had worked to arrange all so. Yet
still there was time. And more time, until all of time for all
contingencies, but one, had lapsed. All her bated, happy
expectancy evaporated more slowly than second by second.
And she sat, then, patiently abandoned. Time wrung itself of
its smallest parts, and she was too numbed, too absenced from
herself, to feel them. Even the last contingency of death
could not be as solitary.

The door opened. And he stood there. And the bitterly,
stinging, very slow slap, the keen, sudden rawness of all the
absenced, wrung moments of time, gathered themselves and
smacked her, all past moments in one stretched moment
forced open and endlessly punished all of her. Her mind, at
its moment of bated release, was released into sudden, raw
pain. The pain tore aside the gathering smile, and left her face,
and her emotions, blank.

He was speaking, trying to speak, and she could not hear.
He was drunk, he was trying to love, he was lovable, and all

she could see was a lout. How greedily she had given her love, how anxiously he had taken it. And in love and lovingness she greedily gave him more and more love. And in all of those empty, waiting hours, he had turned it all into pain. So spend-thrift of all the given love, he was now a stranger too stupid and too selfish to cherish the love she had hoarded for some-one to love. He was abject, and contrite, and still talking.

'I'm sorry you're not dead,' she said, and her voice was so near a frightened whisper that he could hear no accent. 'I'm sorry you're not dead,' she said again, 'then I could still love you.'

There was no tone at all to her voice, but a cavernous echo of a deep, vacant sorrow. She cared not at all. And it ought to have been everything he wanted. Everything, except made of such sorrow. He felt love for her, felt frightened for him-self, felt she knew the cruelty of her sorrow, and would not stop it, was indifferent to his need for guilt, for a rush, for a consumating rush, of guilt. And its possibilities of forgiveness, of expurgation.

'You know you're hurting me,' he said, and she looked startled. And in saying so he knew he did feel hurt, and knew it was a reflected shadow of the pain she had suffered. But she released no energies he could respond to. And he had to get anger, or contempt, or even pity. Just turning away, walking out, now, and the void would never leave his mind, would never stop sucking his energies into its neurotic, endless collapse.

He searched his pockets for money, took some out, and laid it on the table. She reached and took the money, looked at it, and tucked it into her sleeve.

'I deserve more,' she said.

'But I'd be destitute.'

'So what.'

And there, from that accidental kindness, he began to find his own forgiveness. He started to check his money again, stopped himself, and emptied his pockets onto the table.

'I don't want it,' she said. 'You'll need it for yourself.'

'You don't know what I need,' he shouted. And his mind was alive with a gratitude to her, and a contempt for her, that she'd never know. Then he quickly turned and left the room.

He spent the rest of the night sleeping in a disused graveyard.

Its solemn headstones aroused his reverence for the darkness and the cold and the make-believe of life. Without the whisky he would not have been able to sleep.

He arrived at the factory well in time for work. And spent that distant day labouring away guilt and sweat. In the late afternoon he got an advance on his weekly wage. Day by day, week by week, until pennies accumulated into savings, the bought books were read, and it was time again to purchase an earned, more fertile, temporary freedom.

He used it, alone, and tried to use it wisely; to read, to understand, to edge himself towards his own liberation, his own control of himself and his direction in life. And often he thought of the girl, often found himself lost in memories of her, and pined and grieved for her. And sometimes in his mind he would visit her memory, like, exactly like, visiting a grave. Often he thought of her beauty, of the beauty that made him make love to her in his dreams, and in his fantasies, and often he dreamed of meeting her anew when both were wiser, but as fresh, as innocent, as they first had been, months and months before, when they were, intensely, young.